THE GOGMAGOG CIRCUS

Short Story Collections
by Garry Kilworth

'The best short story I've read for many years.'
J.G. Ballard writing about
'Sumi Dreams of a Paper Frog'

The Songbirds of Pain

In the Country of Tattooed Men

Hogfoot Right and Birdhands

Moby Jack and other Tall Tales

The Fabulous Beast

Tales from the Fragrant Harbour

Blood Moon
(a novella and eight short stories)

Elemetal Tales

Dark Hills, Hollow Clocks

In the Hollow of the Deep-Sea Wave
(a novella and six short stories)

The Best Short Stories of Garry Kilworth

The Ragthorn
(a novella written with Robert Holdstock)

THE GOGAMAGOG CIRCUS

Garry Kilworth

The Alchemy Press

Published by
The Alchemy Press, Staffordshire, UK
www.alchemypress.co.uk

Contents

Acknowledgements

Giant © Garry Kilworth 1993. Originally published in *In the Country of Tattooed Men* (HarperCollins)

God's Cold Lips © Garry Kilworth 1979. Originally published in *Aries 1* edited by John Grant (David and Charles)

The Goatboy and the Giant © Garry Kilworth 1979. Originally published in *Fantasy Stories* edited by Mike Ashley (Robinson)

The Head © Garry Kilworth 2021. Originally published in *The Alchemy Press Book of Horrors 3* edited by Peter Coleborn and Jan Edwards (The Alchemy Press)

The Sleeping Giants © Garry Kilworth 1990. Originally published in *Dark Hills, Hollow Clocks* (Methuen)

All other stories are original to this collection © Garry Kilworth 2023

A goblin, tall as a skyscraper, shambled by.
'Be careful what you wish for,' he moaned.

Anonymous

The Head

'You've made a right cock-up of this. You there, mate?'
    'Yes, Pete.'
    'Where exactly are you?' His voice had lost the censure now.
    We were communicating by satellite phone, my emergency contact with the outside world.
    'I'm not sure,' I said. 'I was heading south-east. You can get the position from my signal, can't you?'
    'And you ran the *Aphro* into a bloody reef?'
    'Hey, it's me who should be having the hissy fit. It was night, man. The wind was howling so loud I didn't hear the breakers. The yacht's a dog's breakfast. So, would you please move your arse and come and get me.' Pete was a brilliant sailor, thank God. 'But listen, I don't want anyone but you to know what's happened. You know how important this is to me. I need to get to Hawaii on my own, without any modern navigational devices, otherwise the media will have a field day.'
    'Tangaroa wasn't much help, was he?' Pete asked, with a surprising lack of sarcasm.

~~~

Before setting out for Hawaii, I'd told Pete what I'd done. Tangaroa's carving was up on the prow, but I'd also placed alongside him one of Maui, the trickster god.
    Pete had said, 'You're having me on. Tangaroa's a heavy. You're making him stand next to that little cut-

up Maui? How's that going to work?'

I have a fondness for the trickster god. 'Maui's more interesting. Mate, I love the story where he changed heads with his wife to walk through a village, just to get a reaction – villagers gawping or laughing like dolphins. Anyway, you're no more use than Tangoroa. You have to come and get me.'

'What about all the gear? And what happens to me?'

I sighed with impatience. 'I'm not expecting you to sail blind. Come with the minimum that you need to find your way and we'll leave the stuff here. We can always collect it at a later date, if necessary. And as for you, I'll drop you off somewhere before I reach Hawaii.'

It was Pete who gave with the heavy sigh now. 'With mates like you, who needs –'

'Yes, I know,' I interrupted him. 'If the position was reversed, you know I would do the same for you. Listen, you'll have to use *Circe*. It's got to be the twin sister of the *Aphrodite*. We can change the name on the way to Hawaii.'

'Listen, I'm not hanging over the edge of a boat at sea, painting a new fuckin' name on it.'

'I'll do it.'

'Too right, you will.'

We had been friends for half a lifetime, having gone to the same school together, and then into business as partners in a boat building firm.

'All right. I'll leave Silv in charge here. However, it's going to take over a week to get to you. Can you survive all right? Water? Food? Shelter?'

'I'm good,' I said. 'Don't rush it. If something happens to you, we're really stuffed.'

'No worries.'

'And don't even dob me into Silvia. I don't want anyone to know about this, even my wife. Say you're going to Perth to sell the *Circe*. By the time we come back, it'll be the *Aphrodite*.'

'You'll have to doctor the log, mate.'

'Too right.'

~~~

There was a camera strapped to the mast. A video diary of the voyage was obviously a must for any future lectures. It had always been an ambition of mine to be invited to address the golden three – the Australian Geographic Society, the Royal Geographical Society, the National Geographic Society.

'September 23rd, 2013. The direction of the ocean swell, certain stars embedded in the darkest sky you could imagine, and scattered cloud banks to port tell me I'm somewhere west of the Solomon Islands. Now, it would probably be more authentic if I were a Kiwi,' I said, one hand on a stay and half-facing the camera, 'but I'm an Aussie. I'm not a Maori, not even a New Zealander, but I am passionate about the Polynesian migrations and the bravery of those early islanders who criss-crossed the Pacific in their twin-hulled pahis looking for a new life elsewhere. It's my intention to emulate the voyages of those sea-faring peoples using the same navigational aids.'

I stared out over the vast ocean, giving the camera a profile angle.

'Those wonderful navigator kings set off over this vast ocean, voyaging from atoll to atoll, from island to island, with no charts or instruments, and even without any knowledge of where they were going or what they would find once they got there. Can you imagine such courage? Bamboo craft with pandanus, crab-claw sails carrying families numbering up to a hundred people on each craft, perhaps in convey, emigrating from their birthplace, shooting out over the wide Pacific, the greatest of earth's oceans.'

I turned back to face the camera again. You need to keep changing position, I'm told, in order to retain the audience's attention.

'They left the island of their birth because of overcrowding or rivalry between princes, carrying taro and coconuts, and picking up flying fish and small squid on the way. On board, besides the humans, were dogs, pigs and domesticated birds. No doubt also a rat or two, or three or four, or maybe more.'

I grinned to reinforce this attempt at light humour.

'And how did they find their way, because they didn't just drift around until they hit land? Well, as I've said, no charts or instruments, just the gifts of the natural world. They used the direction of the ocean swells, the paths of the stars, the colour and temperature of the water, the sun, moon and prevailing winds. In order to find a new island they searched the sky for a cloud with a greenish tinge to its base, indicating that down below was a reflecting lagoon. They would put a pig in the water, whose marvellous snout would pick up scents from land miles and miles away and swim towards it. They would follow the direction of sea birds that they knew were looking for a place to nest. They picked up hints from flotsam: palm leaves and other flora.'

Oh, they were a canny set of mariners, those Polynesians, who had no written language. And what joyous warm-wind voyages they made, yes, anxious ones, but full of hope for a new life on a fresh new island. They danced, they sang, they saw the wonders of the blue world – whale sharks perhaps, dolphins, massive lion's mane jellyfish, manta rays – they sailed under skies encrusted with diamonds, the roof of their voyaging. Stories would be told around the fires at night and love affairs and marriages would spice their free hours. There would be rivalries, there would be fights, there would be deaths, but it was life on a tiny floating island.

I went back and turned off the camera and stared at the direction of the swell, and took the tack suggested by the Pacific marine expert I'd talked to before leaving Darwin. Not exactly my expertise, but what the hell. There was also the colour of the waves and the temperature of the water to take into consideration but I'm no 'Feeler of the Sea' as those *kahunas* were called, so these were not prime nav aids for me. Instead, I waited for the night and the star paths to appear. The Southern Cross and companions were much more reliable. I had a modern copy of the ancient Polynesian compass rose of winds, which I didn't consider cheating since the early mariners used it. I suppose in the old days they didn't have written words on the rose, but they would have learned from their grandfather what each thorn was pointing to.

Once more I stared up at the firmament and got a bit emotional, which always turns to lyrical with me trying to express my feelings.

'*Oh, bright star, would I were as steadfast as thou art!*'

Was that Wordsworth or Keats? It didn't matter.

I remained gazing on a sky encrusted with bright stars. They took my breath away, those distant suns, especially out here where the light pollution was nonexistent. I looked for the single diamond that I needed to fix on and then waited for others to rise, one after the other, so that I could follow their path and find the direction of my destination: Hawaii.

Thoughts of those incredible mariners still flowed through my mind when I went off to my berth.

Those early Polynesians couldn't write but they had incredible memories. They could accurately recount any voyage on a crab-clawed canoe that took them through an unexpected odyssey. That was real navigation.

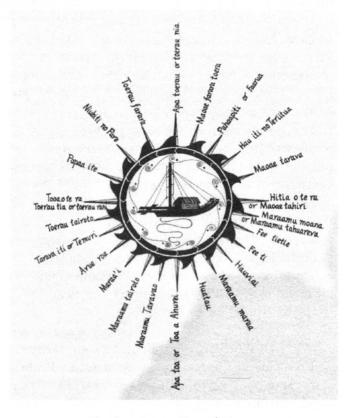

So here I was, in my modern yacht, eschewing the use of satellite devices, or any other modern form of finding my way over the Pacific. At first, all I felt was exhilaration. There's nothing like being barefoot on the warm deck of a sailing boat, cutting through blue water, the wind impregnating the jib and the mainsail, the sun scattering diamonds on the surface of the sea. I could feel the sun on my browned body, smell the salty spindrift in my beard. Free. Free as dolphin, or a frigate bird. This was real life, not dealing with shitty paper in an office, or even with the physical work of boat building. Standing behind the wheel on a sloping deck, shooting out into the unknown. Hell, it filled your whole body with the intense pleasure of experiencing a great passage.

Silvia would sometimes ask me whether this or that would make me happy. 'Once we get the new house, will that make you happy?' I didn't believe in happiness as something you bought and kept, like a flash car. Happiness is fleeting, ephemeral, will-o'-the-wisp. It touches you with light fingers, then it's gone up into the ether. I rarely got that feeling while on land, but out here, with the vast vault of the blue sky above and seemingly borderless ocean stretching to infinity all around, happiness came as passing birds on wings of joy.

It was surely how those early Polynesians must have felt, embarking on a journey into the unknown over the earth's largest ocean. I wanted to be like them, do like them, and maybe even come across an uninhabited island I could claim for myself on the way. An adventure in the later years of my life.

And what I got for myself, was a shipwreck on a coral reef.

~~~

I managed to get ashore with quite a few of my stores and possessions, but because I had set out without electronic aids I had no means of knowing *exactly* where I was. At that point in time I wasn't greatly alarmed. I did have the satellite phone terminal, which was for a dire emergency only (I'm not *totally* crazy), but the camera containing my precious videos was still on the wreck, which was half out of the water. I decided I could get that later, once Pete got here. If in the meantime it went under or got damaged by a storm, I still had the log which I carried always in my backpack. I would need some sort of record of the voyage when I got to Hawaii.

My latest star-path reckoning was that I was somewhere near the Micronesian Islands, specifically the southernmost island, Guam. I had seen two Red-tailed tropicbirds heading north-west – and they surely wouldn't be far from land? The terminal gave me a position, of course, but without charts that position just told me I was somewhere in the middle of the Pacific.

Past the sands I found a beach shack. It was one of those beachcomber or surfer's huts made mainly out of sea-bleached driftwood with a palm-leaf roof, and decorated with shells and coral. Inside, the furniture, such as it was, had been knocked together again out of driftwood or local wood, but seemed quite sturdy, mostly bound together with strips of tree bark and raffia. There were even pictures on the walls, faded pages of photographs cut from magazines, of Polynesian outriggers, and there was one of a marlin hanging from a fisherman's line.

Someone had lived here, though a quick survey of

the island revealed that it now seemed deserted, despite the fact that the shack looked as if it had been vacated at a moment's notice.

The island was not part of an atoll, but a single green smudge on a lapis lazuli sea. It was about a mile long and half-a-mile wide, jungled interior, with signs of animal and bird life. I had trained myself in survival techniques in the event of just such an accident. I had the means of making fire and a small solar-powered desalination unit in case the rain failed me. I would not be wholly comfortable, but in the last resort I would – *inshallah,* as a friend would have it – be able to signal any passing vessel in an emergency.

Besides, I told myself, the oceans of the world are full of craft these days, especially pleasure craft like that wreck I had left on the reef. Some seas you couldn't sail without running into them when you wanted solitude.

On the second morning I was scanning the horizon with my binoculars when an object along the foreshore caught my eye. It was a mound of something quite dark. I couldn't quite make it out with the heat haze, but it appeared to be an item that had been washed up. From the wreck? I didn't remember leaving anything of use behind, not of that size, anyway. I shrugged and put the binoculars down. I would go an investigate later but for the rest of the day I wanted to fish and maybe hunt for fresh food. There were plenty of coconuts around, but meat or fish would be welcome. It did occur to me, however, that there were no strong currents or waves in the lagoon. Plenty out beyond the reef, but the lagoon was calm and placid. So how did such an object wash up so high on the beach? Then I thought, maybe it had been there when I arrived and I just hadn't seen it before that morning.

Towards the evening, I set out to walk along the beach.

As I got closer to the thing which had intrigued me earlier, my stomach suddenly began to churn. I slowed my pace, unable at first to believe what I could see. Finally, I came to a full stop some thirty metres from the object. I felt very uneasy and not a little bewildered. There on the sands, covered with small red pelagic crabs and its hair matted with strands of seaweed, was a human head. It had very long black hair which ran in thick knotted strands well below the roughly severed neck. The face was skywards, staring at the perpetual cloud that hovered over the island, the nose a great arching ridge. But the one aspect of the Head that filled me with queasiness was its size. It was at least three times larger than any natural human head. Had a lengthy time in the water swelled it to its present ugly proportions?

The thing about being on or near the equator is that there's no twilight. One minute it's daylight, the next it's night. No comforting gentle slip through the gloaming, one into the other. As I hurried back to the beach shack, I stumbled and faltered in my efforts to put distance between myself and the monstrous *thing*. I could hardly breathe. Flying foxes - fruit bats - flapped over me on their way to roost in the palms, creating a thrashing din. Somewhere out in the darkness a pig squealed and set my heart racing even faster. Finally, I made the shack and leapt up the wooden steps into the safety of four walls.

Once two or three whiskies had gone down, I managed to rationalise my fears. Why was I being so stupid? I hadn't even checked to see if the Head had been made of flesh. It could have come from a polystyrene model of some kind, possibly having been tossed or fallen from a cruise liner. That was a much more realistic scenario than an actual human head. A giant manikin? Of course. I laughed and turned down the lamp. I had been wasting power to keep my mind from being unhinged. Absolutely pathetic. By the time I went to bed I was almost completely myself again. Not comfortable, but calmer. I finished the bottle, which had only been a third full when I started.

In the middle of the night I woke with wide eyes and stared at a cockroach travelling across the moonlit windowsill.

Why were there crabs all over the Head if it wasn't flesh?

Once morning arrived, I knew I had to go to the Head again. Feeling a lot braver in the bright sunlight, I ran over all sorts of other possibilities in my mind and these began to settle my anxiety. As I approached the Head, from a distance I could see it had rolled over to one side and was now facing me. Perhaps some animal had nudged it in the night? A pig or large lizard? Then once again I slowed my pace. I realised it was now higher up the beach than before, and the sand leading down to the lagoon was showing marks where it had travelled. The hair had left striations on either side of a shallow trench. The crabs were gone but the large-boned skull was still decorated with weed.

Then a shrill noise came from the mouth of the Head.

I turned and ran with all the speed I could urge from my shaking legs back to the shack again.

What was happening here? Had the sound actually come from the Head? I knew from my days of photographing birds in the wild that they could effectively throw their voices. You think a bird is in one bush and it turns out to be in another a few metres away. There might even have been a living creature inside the Head's mouth, but what that could be I had no idea. All I could keep telling myself was that it wasn't possible that the Head could speak.

That night the air felt heavy and oppressive. I knew what was coming. Two hours later a tropical storm attacked the island, filling the sky with sheet and forked lightning. Thunder smashed through the darkness and the crashes came one after the other with a physical force that shook the island to its subsea roots. Rain hammered on the palm-leaf roof and soon forced its way through, making pools on the floor. A tropical storm is nothing like those in temperate regions. The noise is unrelentingly ear-shattering and painful. My head hurt as each bang punched the belly out of the sky. It carried out its usual frustrating cycle, moving away to the distant horizon where I witnessed a scores of jagged strikes all at one time, then returning to hammer the island.

Finally, just before dawn, it went far away out to sea, to harass any shipping.

In the middle of it all I tried to contact Pete, which was utterly foolish because I got nothing but white noise and static. In the morning the beach was littered with rubbish. Plastic oddments and other manmade crap covered the sands. There were molluscs and fish too, that had been caught too close to the water's edge and so flung up onto the shore.

Of course, I told myself, that's how the Head got washed up! A tremendous tropical storm. There were many such wild tempests in the Pacific. And when I used my binoculars, I could see that the giant Head had vanished from the beach. Probably washed out to sea again. Relief flooded through me. It had gone. It had gone. I wasn't crazy. I could settle down, read one or two of the books from the previous owner's shelves. As I said, it seemed he or she had left in a great hurry. There were cans of food in the cupboards and signs of once-fresh food that had been devoured by the ants and cockroaches and anything else that managed to squeeze through cracks.

I was comfortable with life on the island until I came across a passage in a book on Polynesian mythology.

It was believed that there were many supernatural dangers facing those stranded on unfamiliar islands. One of them was the Head of the giant Ulupoka, severed in a battle with the sky god Rangi. It roamed the sands of certain islands, bringing disaster and death. The Head found its way to a human and its bite on the neck, or even the feet, was fatal. It could mimic any sound and would attract an unwary man by copying the sound of a dog or pig. The Head could smell the presence of seafaring men on its shore. Mingling with the sea-bottom odour of drying weed, shellfish and crustaceans coming from an exposed reef, the thick cloying perfume of trumpet blooms, the sometimes-unbelievable stench of rotting mud in the mangrove swamps. It could smell groin sweat, oiled skin and hair, and the stale breath of a lost sailor. When the Head was scuttling and creeping over the landscape, palm-rats sensed the presence of evil and stiffened in their climb. Birds in the frangipani trees stared down with fearful eyes at the strange tracks left upon the coral sands. It seemed the Head travelled from island to island, borne by the waves, ever seeking fresh victims.

'*Fuck!*' I slammed the book down on the rickety table.

I stared out of the window at what was left of the dear old *Aphrodite* and studied the big ocean waves crashing round it on the reef.

A Polynesian giant? A fucking fairy tale? This was a hoax. Someone was screwing with me. I had a good idea who it was, too. The bloody owner of the chair I was sitting in. The man who built this salt-stained sun-bleached wooden hovel. He had fashioned some sort of model and was using it to fuck with my mind. What kind of sick bastard would do a thing like this? Maybe someone with a grudge against rich white yachtsmen who had the audacity to make a landfall on his island? *His* island!

I could hear his voice in my head.

Who did they think they were, these Johnny-come-lately Europeans, taking over his ocean? Going where they pleased without a by-your-leave? He would make them wish they or their ancestors never left the shores of Europe.

I leaned back in the creaking chair and almost toppled over, but my blood was up. I would find that bastard islander and make him wish he'd never left the place where he was born. I filled my backpack with water, biscuits, and sun-dried beef, grabbed a hat and a machete, and set out to scour the whole landscape, inch by inch. Although I had already done a cursory inspection of the hinterland there was an area of high igneous rock in the centre of the rainforest, the island being of volcanic origin. Some of the rocks had been carved into strange figures and perhaps a cave had been hollowed out. He could be hiding in that area, or maybe even in the rainforest itself, keeping one step ahead of me?

I went to the rocky area first but I was so unsettled

and twitchy the stone carvings gave me the frights. There was an eerie feeling about the place so I left after a cursory inspection. I didn't want the islander, if he was a Polynesian, to complain later that I had been desecrating a place where his ancestors or gods were held sacred. I wanted no excuse to get in the way of my righteous wrath.

After four hours I was exhausted and trudged back to the shack. Some of the rainforest had been thicker than I first thought. I had to hack my way through thorny acacias and lawyer vines, which left my forearms bleeding and my pants shredded. There were great hanging loops of those tree-parasites, lianas, as thick as my thigh, and the trees grew so close in places it was impossible to squeeze between them. There were boggy places too, especially where the mangroves grew. I hadn't found the perpetrator of that foul practical joke and I was completely depressed by the whole episode. All I wanted to do now was get off this hellhole and out into the Pacific again, where the air is fresh and the scent is of salt water on a cedar deck.

I got to the shack about five o'clock and rummaged in one of the cupboards. I had seen a bottle of liquid in there not long after arrival and on sniffing it I knew it was kava, the favourite hooch of Polynesian islanders. It's supposed to relieve anxiety and induce feelings of relaxation and calm. I needed all of those and sat on the steps of the porch, without even taking off my backpack. I sat quietly sipping away and staring out to sea hoping to find a yacht on the horizon.

Then...

...the Head came out of the surf and up the beach with incredible speed.

It used its hair like flails, which it flung forward to

grip on logs and coral lumps, anything, even the raffia bedstead I used as a sun lounger. It came tumbling forward with an intensely eager look on its immense and pockmarked features, the cavernous nostrils flaring, the dark eyes wide and glinting with anticipation, the thick brutish lips curled back, its tongue-tip protruding between the two rows of even yellow teeth. It was huge and hideous, and the shock of its swift progress was almost petrifying. I froze but only for a second before leaping up and snatching the machete from the step beside me.

It was almost upon me, its wide mouth open, its teeth clattering, when I struck it a blow on its forehead. The slavering eagerness vanished from its expression and it screamed, shrilly, loudly. Terrified, I managed to hit it once more and its high annoyance turned to pure fury. It lunged at me and gripped my shirt for a second, but I grabbed a handful of sand and flung it into those red-rimmed eyes, forcing it to release me. I ran in panic for the trees.

My shaking legs carried me straight back into the rainforest and along the narrow track I had cut for myself earlier that day. The Head tried to follow me, but its momentum was halted when its hair became tangled in the thick undergrowth. The fiend let out a bellow of rage before retreating, leaving strands and red clumps of its scalp hanging from bushes and tree bark.

Whimpering with shock and disbelief, I made my way back to the middle of the island to hide. There I stayed for three days. I drank dirty water from a pool, which made me retch, and ate berries that I was sure were going to kill me, but thankfully only gave me stomach cramps. In the night I went as high as I could up the jagged volcanic rock, hoping that if the Head did manage to reach this place it would have trouble climbing. Sleep evaded me most of the time, both through the fear and the pain from sharp stones. In the end I was so ragged and unwell, I decided to go back and face my fate. With the machete still in my possession I set off hoping to find the Head gone.

When I reached the edge of the rainforest, I peered out and to my immense relief I could see a familiar yacht moored beyond the reef. There was a yellow dinghy floating in the shallows. Pete had arrived! I could see his footprints leading up to the shack. I almost wept with joy. I had managed to stay alive and now we could kick this infernal island into the past and leave it there for good. I ran to the shack, one eye on the surf for any sign of the monster. The lagoon was clear, however, and nothing lurked there.

'Pete, Pete,' I cried, running up the steps. 'We have to get away from here. We have to —'

Flinging open the door, the next word jammed in my throat.

There he was, my best friend. Or at least there was half of him. Just the legs and part of the torso remained on the blood-soaked floor. The Head looked up from its meal and stared at me as if I were a trespasser. Gore hung from its lips and it quickly licked the filaments away, before going back to eating Pete.

I turned and ran, leaping off the porch. The beach sped under my feet, weary and weak as I was, my strength surging from a well of deep horror. The dinghy took my weight as I flung myself in it and shot out into the lagoon. Once on the *Circe* I cast off. I sailed away from that miserable island and only found time to mourn my friend when that ugly lump of dead coral was safely out of sight below the horizon.

When I believed I was two days away from my destination, I dumped all the electronic equipment overboard. Then I moored on a shoal and changed the name of the vessel from *Circe* to *Aphrodite*. They hailed me as a hero when I hove into Pearl Harbour, and I soaked it up. I soaked it up without a conscience. I deserved that bloody adulation. I had earned it ten times over. I had already mourned my friend on the final leg of the voyage.

Pete was thought to have been lost at sea. He had left Brisbane, ostensibly for Perth, and hadn't contacted a soul since then. On average, two thousand lives are lost annually at sea, so his death was not thought suspicious nor was it investigated. It was widely assumed he had got into difficulties and had gone down with his boat. I mourned him – he was a good mate, a loyal friend – but I didn't do so without being plagued by nightmares.

I still worry that the wreck of the original *Aphrodite* will be discovered, along with my camera containing videos of the voyage to that infernal island. I could be defrocked even now. That particular scenario bothers me only a little, however. The thing that really does upset me is a visit to a wild, lonely shore. Can't do it without a panic attack. I get jumpy and nervous and if Silvia's with me, my dear wife, she sometimes looks at me with deep concern. Then there're the nightmares – when I wake up screaming. She tells me I've changed since the voyage, and she's right. She asks what really happened and I want to reply, 'There are more things in Heaven and Earth, Sylvia…' But I don't.

We live too close to the shore.

A Tale of Two Giants

I was sent by my newspaper to cover the fight. There was to be a battle between two giants. Fortune's wheel was spinning. I had just moved from a provincial paper to the *Regency Gazette* and this would either make me or break me. I didn't fancy being broken so I set my jaw, determined to bring back a good story. I learned that it was Lady Julia Price-Swanson, the Editor-in-Chief's wife who said to her husband, 'Give that new young man a chance. See what he can do. A fresh pen.'

The News Editor, John Scarletti, had taken against me from the start for some reason. As a weak indecisive man, I'm sure he believed I was after his job. I was a long way below him and had a few years of hard work ahead of me, but men like Scarletti are frightened of any subordinate who shows promise. I took it as a compliment that he disliked me and wanted me gone. Anyway, he had protested to Price-Swanson saying a more experienced journalist would be ten times better at covering the story. The Chief remained adamant. I had no idea why his wife, a woman I had never even met, was so keen to see what I could do. Perhaps she just wanted to annoy Scarletti?

Indeed, I was not only keen to progress in the firm, I was desperate. The rent for London lodgings was exorbitant and I had arrived in the city not only penniless but already owing money to various tradesmen – close to twenty-five sovereigns at the time. It is one thing to triumph at an interview where the News Editor, a powerful voice, is against you, but quite another to uproot from a northern town and make a new life in the capital city. New clothes were required for the London scene. A horse was necessary for someone as junior as me in order to reach all parts of the country where a story might be forthcoming. I had to eat and drink with those who could afford better meals than me in order to pick up scandal and inside information on those in the government and in the criminal class. People want to read about the fall of a leading politician – or a multi-murderer.

So here I was, setting off on horseback for Wiltshire, about halfway between the homes of the two giants. I could have hired a coach but the fight was due to take place on Salisbury Plain, and even if was near a highway the roads were terrible in that region. It was over 80 miles from London to the battlefield so I planned to overnight in two inns along the way. I could pick up some gossip from those intending to witness the match between Comoran and Gwendol.

Apart from the usual riff-raff that attend boxing matches and any other so-called sporting event, aristocratic gentlemen are drawn by the opportunity to wager. Estates could be won and lost. Dukes, earls, lords, would go home with more than empty pockets to explain to their wives that they had to move to that pretty little cottage in the country that her cousin Tristram had left her in his will. All grist for the mill, as far as I was concerned.

So, you will be wondering about the two protagonists in the forthcoming fight and why they needed to battle.

Comoran, the shorter of the two by half a yard, was

a Cornishman. It was he who had made St Michael's Mount out of local white granite. He used it as a base from which to raid cattle. With the help of his wife he had carried huge stones out into the sea and formed a tidal island which the locals called *Karrek Loos yn Koos*, or White Rock in the Woodland. Cornelian, his better half, had found herself in trouble when she used the wrong stones while he was asleep. Comoran knocked the contents of her apron, greenstones, to the ground. This pile of rubble is now known as Chapel Rock.

The pair were very proud of the finished article, this tidal retreat, and brooked no criticism of their efforts.

Comoran's rival in the coming contest was Gwendol Wrekin ap Shenkin ap Mynddmawr, called simply Gwendol. Looking at the title he had given himself, I guessed his ancestors came from Wales, but Gwendol lived in Shropshire bordering that fine mountainous country. The hill he was famous for having made was the Wrekin, which stood in an area of flat ground and stuck out like a bump on a man's back. Unlike Comoran's pride and joy, Gwendol's hill was an accident.

The story that my grandmother told me was that Gwendol had a dispute with the town of Shrewsbury and set out with a spadeful of earth to block the River Severn. It was his intention to flood the town and drown its inhabitants. He hadn't gone very far before he met a pedlar, a cobbler who had a pile of worn shoes strung over his shoulders. Gwendol was not the brightest giant in the room and he had forgotten the way to Shrewsbury, so he asked the cobbler which road he should take. When the cobbler, whose family lived in Shrewsbury, found out what was afoot he said to Gwendol, 'Lord, it's a long way to that town. Look,

I've worn out all these shoes walking from it.' Gwendol, as I said, is pretty dimly lit in the attic and gave up his task and dumped the earth where he stood. This became the hill we call the Wrekin. As with Comoran and his wife, there was a smaller mound when Gwendol scraped the mud off his boots and left Ercall Hill behind him as he walked away.

By the by, my research had informed me that Comoran had already killed one giant, a burly monster called Gogamagog.

~~~

That first night I stayed at an inn called The March Hare, in the village of Spalding, a third of the way to my destination. I was lucky to get a room. The place was packed with sporting gentlemen, their grooms and valets. Carriages littered the greensward leading up to the inn and the stables were bursting at the seams with livestock. Like many other horses, my mount had to share a paddock belonging to one of the villagers. I will not mention the price of both the inn and the paddock but I knew I wouldn't see its return in expenses. These wayside halts were ever ready to milk travelling gentlemen who had no choice but to pay the rate that was being asked. Likewise, the supper of rabbit stew and potatoes might just as well have been venison or turtle, considering the cost.

After supper I inveigled my way onto the table of a young man wearing white Cossack pantaloons, a deep-blue fashionable tailcoat, an outlandish stock that kept his head absolutely erect, silk cravat, and tall boots. He was the very mark of sporting man, though quite obviously inclined to dandyism. By his modish appearance I knew he was one of those members of the ton who lived and breathed for the attention of his set.

He would ride to the hounds, be present at shoots at country estates, attend all the fashionable parties and balls, would frequently be found playing *chemin de fer* for high stakes, and he would have hacked in the London parks with beautiful well-bred ladies. I didn't doubt he craved the admiration and envy of his peers and wallowed in the praise of friends who copied his latest artistic folding of the cravat. In other words, he was also a fop. In the ton it was *de rigueur* to be a tulip of fashion as well as a sporting gentleman. You had to look the Corinthian as well as be one.

This swift but accurate appraisal of the young man gave me an idea.

'Excuse me, my dear sir,' I said, 'I wonder if you mind me sharing your table. There doesn't seem to be another space free at this time.'

He pointed with his knife at the chair. 'Sit you down, sir.'

'Thank you.' I settled myself with my glass of port. 'I assume you are going to the match between the giants?' I said.

'Who here is not?' he replied, sweeping his fork over the whole assemblage, then stuffing a wadge of pork into his mouth.

'Do you have a favourite? I myself am ignorant of the fighting qualities of both the protagonists.'

Young men with no experience, skill or wisdom always fancy themselves intuitively knowledgeable when it comes to wagering on a winner. 'You would be well advised to place your blunt on the Salopian, sir.' He then regarded my attire closely and added, 'if you have any.'

'Ah, you think I lack money because by the clothes I choose to wear I obviously lack breeding, but the world is in change, sir. One does not need to rely on family wealth to get on in life. In fact, my father is a successful merchant but I shall see none of his money until he passes on.'

'And you yourself are in trade?'

'I sir, am a journalist. I write for a very popular newspaper, the *Regency Gazette*. You may have heard of it? My name is Albert Crabtree.'

I was being ironic. Every man jack in the country knows the *RG* and I saw his eyes widen. Albert was a new acquaintance who wrote the sports columns and was known throughout the kingdom. Men, those who recognised him, stopped him in the street to shake his hand and gush. He was a good fellow to be with in a tavern or an inn as drinks would be offered to him and his companion.

'Of course I have. I take it mainly for the boxing. I am a great follower of the sport. I love a wager. I am Viscount Blythe. Being a journalist, you may have heard of me. I won a great deal of money on a raindrop.' He grinned and then continued. 'There were several raindrops running down a windowpane in my London club – White's – and a number of gentlemen present wagered on which raindrop would reach the bottom of the pane first. Mine won.'

He puffed out his bright yellow waistcoat in pride.

'So,' I said, taking a sip of my port, 'would you be prepared to place a wager on the fight between the giants? I am at your service, my lord.'

A puzzled look came over his face. And then he gave a little laugh.

'You have already told me you do not have the kind of money which would allow you to place a bet with a man of my standing.'

'My lord, I am a journalist. I can make you famous. If you win, I shall make it my business to consult you on many sporting events and my fellow journalists, whether they be reporting on the latest fashion, or anything that requires an opinion from a member of the public, will consult and quote you in their column. Is that your coat on the stand by the parlour door? I see a multitude of capes on the shoulders. It suggests you drive to an inch, sir, and your advice to other young men would be most welcome – were you to win our wager.'

A gleam came into his eyes.

'Ah, you intrigue me, sir. I must admit the prospect does interest me. How will you guarantee that you will carry out your promise?'

I tried to look shocked.

'Trust, my lord. Trust. My word is sacred. How could I write a respected column if it became known that I had welched on a bet? It would be the ruin of me. No, no, my lord, I would honour it to the letter.'

He nodded thoughtfully. 'I hadn't thought about that. All right. How would fifty sovereigns suit you? I have the money with me, so there would be no question of me not paying my dues. However, I have already stated my choice, which is Gwendol. That leaves you the Cornishman. Are you prepared to go with Comoran?'

'I am indeed. Here's my bond.'

He took the proffered hand and gave it a hearty shake.

Thus we were set.

'I'd like to offer you a lift in my curricle,' said the viscount, 'but I can only carry one other and that man is my tiger. I'm sure you understand.'

'Fully. You need your groom and I certainly couldn't replace him. My skill regarding the management of horses is limited to my own nag.'

He smiled. 'I'm sure a man in your position doesn't have anything but a perfectly good riding horse. And should you win, which I very much doubt, you'll be able to buy yourself a hunter. Good luck, sir.'

'And to you, my lord.'

~~~

Now, perhaps I should explain why I was so confident that Comoran would win the fight. If you are not familiar with it, giants battle with each other by throwing rocks at their opponent. They find large stones, boulders even, and stand about five-hundred yards apart to hurl a missile at their adversary. Rough though it sounds, the rules are much the same as the etiquette agreed between two gentlemen duellists. First blood stops the action and the winner walks away having satisfied his honour. A killing blow is to be regretted. Giants and men are equal under the law and as such the winning giant might suffer incarceration if the other combatant received a mortal hit.

Most giants are pretty inaccurate with their chosen weapons. Rocks and stones go everywhere but only occasionally hit the target. Sometimes the fighters exhaust themselves and go home without a definite result. However, I knew something the young lord did not. Comoran was wont to practise hurling rocks at his cousin, the Trencom giant. In fact, his cousin had accidently struck Comoran's wife with a wayward lump of granite and yet they still had the odd mock battle between them. Comoran, therefore, was more likely to be the better thrower than Gwendol. I felt pretty confident of victory. With that in mind I stayed in a grander room at the next inn. No box room over the stables stinking of manure this time, but one with a view of a church whose magnificent steeple pierced the dying sky at the end of the day.

~~~

Next day, arriving at the place where the two giants were to battle, I joined the gathering crowd of watchers on high ground. We could look down on the scene and had a wonderful view of the duel. Glancing round, I sought the viscount and found him quite easily. His yellow waistcoat shone like a lemon amongst a horde of turnips and potatoes. I waved to him and though he hesitated and looked stiff, he did make some sort of gesture to indicate that he knew I was there. Then he turned to his equals and a laugh went up. I guessed from the way his companions' faces swivelled round in my direction that he had made me a figure of fun. Probably he was bragging about how he was going to win a remarkable wager, even more remarkable than his raindrop triumph.

An hour later we witnessed the two giants coming from opposite directions. Gwendol ambled down from the North. He was a gangling figure, with long arms and legs, not particularly muscular or strong looking. However he was taller than his opponent, now stamping up from the South.

Comoran was square and solid. There was not an ounce of fat on him. Thick muscled arms and legs, the latter driving him forward, were attached to massive chest and hips. He had been known to crush enemy ships with those hands, both of which had six fingers. His toes too, came in half-dozens. The first were probably good for throwing missiles, the second for gripping the earth when he flung them.

Both creatures bellowed when they saw each other and made hideous faces. One might almost compare them with school children in the way they shouted insults and distorted their features. Behind each of them were large bands of followers and countrymen, Cornish folk trailing Comoran and Salopians keeping up with Gwendol. Some were on horseback, some were in carriages, and the vast majority on foot. They cheered their favourites when the giants went through their battle dances, each different in its way, clearly meant to intimidate the enemy. Each combatant had several carts driven by farmers carrying large rocks, some as big as a wine vat.

Finally, after a great deal more gesturing and roaring, Gwendol reached down and picked a chunk of quartz from a cart and lobbed it towards Comoran. His long arm acted like a medieval trebuchet siege weapon, flinging the missile high in the air, to come down almost vertically on its target. It fell short by twenty yards.

We on the high ground cheered, the Salopians yelled in delight while the Cornish jeered and sneered and began doing the Furry Dance. Comoran's style was to throw a lump of granite about ten feet off the ground, hoping to hit his opponent's groin. His first missile passed through Gwendol's legs and shattered a waggon beyond, which had the Cornish hooting like mad.

And so it continued, with huge pieces of Welsh mountain flying through the air from the Shropshire giant, and massive chunks of Cornish cliff whistling from the giant who built St Michael's Mount. As the morning went on and there were no direct strikes, the giants began to visibly tire. At midday their rocks were landing in the ground halfway between them. The only problem with this was that Stonehenge lay midway between the two contestants. Boulders were striking the standing stones and it wasn't long before the first trilithon toppled over in the manner of skittles.

The crowd standing with me were aghast at the damage these giants were causing to a national treasure. But who could stop them? They were still full of fighting fury and any intervention might be disastrous. Just when we thought it was all over and the pair would go home without a winner, they both marched towards one another, meeting in the Stonehenge circle. They used the bluestones first, picking them out of the ground and tossing them like cabers at each other. When this was a failure they started pushing over the remaining sarsens, trying to get one to fall on their opponent. I watched in awe as Gwendol used his foot on a great monolith, sending it towards his enemy. Unfortunately for him, and happily for the other giant, it fell a few inches short.

Then when the Shropshire giant was almost directly under a trilithon, Comoran kicked one of the uprights away. The massive lintel slid down an upright and landed on Gwendol's right foot. The giant who had made the Wrekin, fell to the ground screaming so loud it hurt our ears. The Cornish contingent cheered and danced, knowing their fighter had taught those midland bastards which was the better county. Then they crowded around their exhausted hero and led him away, southwest, towards the land they loved best.

Gwendol was helped to his feet by a group of men and a mobile windlass. His foot looked mangled but he limped away accompanied by his followers. The contest was all over and I had won my bet, but I did wonder what the government department responsible for antiquities was going to do about our now scattered prehistoric monument.

I went to find my macaroni and to collect my winnings.

The viscount was just about to get into his curricle.

He turned and sneered. 'What do you want?'

'I believe you owe me money, my lord,' I retorted.

'As to that, my lowlife friend, you may whistle a merry tune. You might be a well-known journalist but I, sir, am a viscount.'

'You will remember,' I reminded him, 'that if you won the wager I promised to raise your profile in both the sporting world and the world of fashion.'

He looked down his nose at me while his tiger walked out of earshot staring into the middle distance.

'And?'

'And if I can do one, I can do the reverse. How would you like to wake up tomorrow morning to find you are a villain?'

His face went crimson with anger.

'You wouldn't dare. What would you say about me? That I didn't pay a gambling debt? I shall just deny it was ever made.'

'Oh, I shall just make something up,' I said, casually. 'We journalists do that all the time, my lord. Something about your past as a rake, perhaps? No, that would probably raise your profile amongst your set. I know, I'll make it a vague scandal involving your family. I can find the names. Something that will have people saying: 'Well whether there's any truth in it is not for me to say, but I always think there's no smoke without a fire.' Or perhaps a story about your illegitimacy. Not a bastard, my lord? Oh so hard to prove, though.'

While our conversation was in progress, two scruffy urchins, hand-in-hand, stopped to stare hard at the viscount's belly.

The girl said, 'Look at 'is vest, Jamie. It's bewtiful. 'E must be what they call a toolip.'

The smaller child, a boy, peered at the bright yellow waistcoat and replied, 'More like a daff-ee-dil then, eh?'

The pair them sauntered off and a smile blossomed in my bosom.

Blythe stood there smouldering for at least two minutes more, then finally he reached into his curricle. I did think for one moment his hand might have emerged with a pistol in it, but there were still many people around and his tiger had returned to the curricle. Soon, I had fifty sovereigns weighing down my saddlebag. The viscount left, whipping his pair of matched greys. The poor beasts were getting what he wanted to give me and I pitied them.

Childishly, I couldn't help yelling after him, 'Next time, stick to raindrops.'

~~~

The mess the giants had left of Stonehenge was hushed up. No one wanted word of it to reach the continent. The French would jeer at us, the Prussians would maintain that the authenticity of the monument was now in question and the Italians would simply state that there was nothing of real antiquity to see in Britain. The two giants were ordered to put the stones back in their rightful places. The trouble was, although there were paintings and drawings, one could never be sure the right sarsen upright in a trilithon had been paired with the correct lintel. It appeared to me that one or two were still lying on their backs, but that was no business of mine.

The Sleeping Giants

Back in the time when what was what, and before things changed, there was a miller who fathered five sons and one daughter. Now, the five sons had several choices concerning what to do with their lives, from joining the army as trumpet majors, to running away to sea, to becoming the mayor of a town. The miller's daughter, however, had but two. She could stay and help her parents run the mill, or she could marry and help someone else's son run his farm. *This* miller's daughter, whose name was Jill, wasn't having either of those. She informed everyone she was going out in the world to build her *own* mill. Her brothers laughed, her parents wailed, but Jill thumbed her nose, and set off one dawn when the flour was like powdered stars, still in peaceful heaps on the loft floor.

On the way along the road, she met a wolf.

'So, what's all the hush and rurry?' he spoonered. Jill ignored him, and since his curiosity was aroused the wolf fell in behind her, and they continued along the winding road together.

Soon they came to a wooden bridge across a stream. As Jill and the wolf were crossing a troll leaped from the grassy bank to bar their way.

The startled wolf jumped and then put his paw on his chest. 'Don't *do* that!' he said.

'Where are you two going?' snarled the troll.

Jill brushed him aside in contempt. The troll looked at the wolf, who shrugged, and the Scandinavian immigrant fell in with them, intrigued by this strange girl with a faraway look in her eyes.

The trio entered a deep dark wood, where a wodwo had its home in a hollow log. It jumped out at them as they passed along a narrow path and the wolf shrieked and almost fainted.

'What am I?' cried the wodwo, this being the only question he had ever wanted answered since finding himself in a squirrel's drey some seventeen summers ago. He had seen his reflection in a pool: a lump of clay with bits of twigs and feathers sticking out of his head; grasses growing from his ears (if they *were* ears); pebbles and pieces of bark and bracken and other stuff elsewhere on his form.

Everyone completely ignored him.

The wodwo tagged on behind until they came to a dragon stretched across the path.

'Why don't you join us?' suggested the wolf but the dragon declined, saying that she didn't like the look of the lump of green mud with twigs for hair, which left the wodwo muttering, 'A green? I didn't know I was a green. What's a *green* anyway?'

Finally, the whole group reached a long fertile valley where a giant lay on its side, fast asleep. They walked the whole length of this enormous creature until they reached its head in the late evening. The wind from its slow regular breathing lifted Jill's hair and made it stream out behind her, yellow and long.

'This is it,' she said, putting down her pack.

'This is what?' chorused the others.

'This is where we build the windmill. You, wolfie, go and borrow some tools. You with the twigs, go and look for a large round flat stone in the river. Make sure it's smooth and when you find one, bore a hole through the middle. Troll, you can help me stitch some sails out of these sheets I've brought.'

Soon the place was an ants' hill of activity. The wolf felled timber with an axe borrowed from a woodsman and the troll sawed them up into long yellow planks. Jill began nailing the planks together. The wodwo took it on himself to do intricate work, like the frames for the sails, at the same time asking curious onlookers if they knew what he was.

Before long the sleeping giant's deep and steady breath, which smelled of freshly cut herbs and ground peppers, was turning the great sails of Jill's windmill. Farmers began to move to the valley and the fields started to yield wheat, maize, barley and oats.

The giant slept on.

By the following year the windmill was grinding corn and producing fine flour which sold throughout the land. Jill adopted the wodwo, but the wolf (poor devil) was bitten by a strange man at full moon and had to be shot with a silver bullet. The troll became a full partner in the mill.

A passing pilgrim helped the wodwo begin compiling a list of all the things he was *not*, hoping one day to reach an object that could not be accounted for.

Soon the valley began to fill with people.

First came the real estate agents, and the lawyers.

Then a swarm of tinkers and pedlars. Then the tradesmen and shopkeepers. A schoolhouse was built, and a church.

Then came a doctor, who was also an insurance salesman, followed by a banker, some oddly assorted police, and a man who set up a private sanatorium for broken-down actors.

The postal services moved in.

An old tramp made his home in the giant's hair.

A clocktower was raised as high as the giant's shoulder.

A town hall was erected and a mayor elected.

Homeless aristocrats began to drift in.

So, around Jill's windmill, the sails of which were turned by the giant's dependable breath, a whole town sprang up. In time there were even refuse collecting services.

The giant slept on, surrounded by beautiful buildings and dreaming spires.

An artist sketched the town, and a poet came there to die. The townspeople built bridges over the giant's limbs, great sweeping arches that melted into roads. One side of the giant, where the mill stood, became known as Windy Streets. The other, behind the giant's back, was called Calm Hills.

Soon the town became a city and trains were invented. Cars came along and streetlights and garage walls and graffiti. The city began to get an overcrowding problem, especially out on the limits where the immigrants tended to settle and where the refugee camps were situated.

Jill retired with the wodwo and troll to a place by the sea, where they opened up a tea shop and a penny amusement arcade. They sold the mill to an enthusiastic intellectual who turned it into a museum. It was painted white, had pretty window boxes, and many visitors came to see its wooden cogs and levers ('In *actual* working order') turned and moved by the sails.

The giant slept on.

In fact, the giant's breath had become a bit of a nuisance. It blew away hats and umbrellas, raised dust and litter, and its constancy was really rather irritating. People preferred to live on the far side of the giant, in Calm Hills, where it was rather more peaceful. The prices of houses in Calm Hills rose steeply, until only the very wealthy could afford to live there.

On Windy Streets, where the giant's snoring breath threw up rubbish and paper, the poorer folks' houses began to deteriorate rapidly. The landlords of these dwellings all lived on the far side of the giant and sent only rent collectors, never maintenance men. After all, *they* did not have to live in decrepit buildings or smell overflowing sewers. Some of them had never seen a rat or a cockroach in their lives.

As properties in Windy Streets fell into disrepair, the larger shops and stores closed down and businesses began to move away. Unemployment rose and there was despair and heartache.

The paint peeled off the windmill and since gangs of knaves roamed the streets looking for trouble, visitors were reluctant to make the journey to the mill anymore. A changeling named Stilty Rump bought the windmill for a song, painted it red, and turned it into a night-club. There was a casino at the back, and a restaurant on the second storey. The power was provided by an electric generator driven by the refurbished sails.

The giant slept on.

There were murders and suicides and theft and bribes, all somehow connected with Stilty's mill, though nothing could be proven. Politicians became involved, police were corrupted, and rival gangs raided the windmill from time to time causing bloodshed. This did not prevent the residents of Calm Hills from coming to Windy Streets in their windproof sedans, to gamble and generally have a good time. Then one blowy evening, when the nightingales were singing in the squares, Stilty Rump was arrested and taken to jail. His reign was over.

Stilty's sons and daughters had been college educated and opened legitimate businesses. They turned the mill into a working model again for the interest and education of school children and overseas visitors. The mill was staffed by long-haired pixies and elves who made wholemeal bread (full of goodness and fibre) which sold to health food shops.

'Windmill Bread' became famous, and the mill attracted many people from foreign lands. City officials were constantly harassed by important visitors, asking why Windy Streets was a ghetto. They pointed out that vitelline taxi drivers still refused to take fares to that part of the city.

So, new honest policemen were drafted in to weed out the rotten ones, and arrests were made amongst the gangland fairy folk. Bad politicians packed their bags and left town.

The giant woke up and went away, taking the ruins of several bridges with him.

The windmill closed and became an historic monument.

Two proposals were put forward regarding the space vacated by the giant. One, that it should be used to rehouse people from the ghetto. Two, that it should become a private golf course for patrons from Calm Hills.

The golf course won.

The windmill became a secret bomb factory for a group of anarchist elves called the Gretalites. The buildings in Windy Streets were finally condemned and the tenants and paupers moved out, most of them heading for the coast to run slot machine arcades in the booming seaside towns. Early one morning in May, when the blossom was pink on the bough, there was a tremendous explosion which blew the windmill to pieces. The whole district was flattened. Landowners sold their acres to the *nouveau riche* from the resorts on the coast, who built inland hotels as quiet retreats away from the hurly-burly of the flourishing ports.

A second giant came along.

Seeing a nice soft patch of green turf in the centre of the city, he lay down to sleep, with his face towards Calm Hills.

His foul exhalations whistled noisily down the driveways of the large mansions owned by wealthy landlords and politicians, stirring the gravel, rattling garage doors and blowing top spray from the garden swimming pools. Tennis court nets were whisked away like chiffon scarves and deck chairs and pool umbrellas decorated the trees. Greenhouses and conservatories were flattened. The panels of expensive fences flew like bats into the evening skies.

The new giant had rotten teeth and bad breath.

Property prices fell overnight to rock bottom and the rich became poor, and the poor became rich. Some might say that was a happy ending if the story stopped here, which of course it never does.

It simply starts again, perhaps with the hotel owner who had five daughters and a son?

Once upon a time...

God's Cold Lips

1

The eyelids hung heavy as shields and opened with great difficulty to reveal a polished sky. The bright yellowness twisted and warped its shape, floating like an amoeba before him, splitting into smaller cells that danced apart, then plunged together again. Finally he managed to focus and turned his face away from the Sun with annoyance, a small growl escaping his throat. The sound worried him but he was feeling too drowsy to follow the thought to a conclusion. He knew that he was not unwell but merely recovering from a long sleep. He lifted his arm slowly and with great effort to his mouth – and tasted fur. *The transmutation had been a success.* Rolling onto his side he began falling into a deep sleep again.

'Switch off the overhead lights,' he heard a voice saying softly. 'Let him rest. Tomorrow his system will have absorbed...' The rest was lost in the humming of his brain. He fell asleep again with the strong smell of sweetstick burning his olfactory lobes.

~~~

He was Adam Marillac – or was he? He certainly wasn't the tiger – that was merely the fur, flesh and bone that housed his soul. He felt nothing like a large cat; he felt like Marillac, swallowed. In fact, he thought, he was neither of these animals. He was an idea, an abstract enthusiasm in another man's mind. An experiment. To be precise, Experiment T3 – the T being Tiger, of course. There had already been a D1 and a B2. They had been children, almost babies, and unaware of their cell rearrangement.

'They had to put your existing cells through a multiplexer – there weren't enough of them to make up the tiger on their own. I trust you're comfortable? Also, there's a silver stud in your ear – an identification disc of sorts. You'll need it later when we come to take you home.'

He dipped his eyelids. It still hurt to move them quickly.

Steen continued: 'We'll let you out into the jungle in a few days – I trust you're ready for it? No worries?'

No worries? Of course he was worried. More than that, he was terrified. The jungle was a thick web of black and green, damp horror. A tiger may be unconcerned with spiders, indifferent to snakes. Adam Marillac was almost insanely terror-struck at the sight of either creature. The thought of them made his throat muscles constrict involuntarily with fear. The jungle was full of snakes and spiders. The jungle was full of all those nightmares that had haunted him through childhood and into maturity.

Childhood had been spent in the usual way: kindergarten, school, university. Marillac tried to remember a single event of his childhood that was not related to one of these institutions – and failed. They took in an infant at four years old and from that point onwards, until the time came to find a job, they smothered the child with a learning administered within the surrounds of plastimetal furnishings and endless banyan buildings. Marillac had only once before stood under the unscreened harshness of a starlit summer sky; had only once throughout manhood sat on dangerously damp meadowgrass in the wild atmospheres of a light breeze; had, that single time, smelled the hostile fumes of wildflowers. The excursion outside the city had been necessary to complete his education and he, like all the others, had been frightened by the weird sounds and the vast openness of the outside world.

But he had promised to live in the environment for which his new body was suited – at least for a time. Six months or so they said – barring accidents. Barring complications. Barring death from inside the tiger, or from without.

It was difficult adjusting to his new role in life, albeit a temporary post. As yet, his body was uncoordinated, and he tended to make foolish mistakes with the heavy limbs. Steen said he would get used to them quite quickly.

But then Steen was no expert on gaining control of an animal's body, a big cat's body – there were no experts. Steen was merely the sponsor for his transmutation. Together they were supposed to be striving to put together a paper – but it was Marillac who was taking all the risks. Steen just sat back and watched, pulling away affectedly on that old-fashioned drug of his.

When Marillac had first realised he was going to become a tiger he had studied the animal, both from books and live in captivity. One thing, a single trait, had endeared tigers to him – they were solitary beasts. Marillac was a loner and always had been. He had been married once but was now divorced. It was the marital state, the togetherness, that had been wrong, not his choice of bride. She had never understood why he left so suddenly.

Now he was really alone, divorced from the human race by a barrier only skin-thick, but impenetrable. Soon he would be entering that terrible jungle, undefended by the technology of Man. It was a sobering thought that he would have to kill, at close quarters, with his bare … claws? … to live.

~~~

They were standing inside the giant gates before which lay the jungles. Nothing stood between himself and the man, but Steen held a stunrod as self-consciously as a new general holds his rank; other pale brittle men stood nearby, arms folded to make sharp triangles. Already Marillac felt alienated, untrustworthy. What did they expect he might do – swing a pawful of dagger-like claws at Steen's head, suddenly? This was all a bit uncalled for, a bit farcical. He even liked Steen a little.

'Well, old chap,' said Steen, swinging the stunrod by his side like a baton, 'hope you don't get too bored. We'll put some cooked meat by the gate each day for a while – you won't feel up to hunting for a bit.' He paused and pulled on his sweetstick, then added: 'It is important, you know. A lot of people will thank you for it later.'

'Or not,' thought Marillac. They wouldn't thank him if the thing was a failure – even if it was just the idea that failed. The breeze was changing direction and he lifted his nose to it. No longer did the sweat of those armpits, or the fumes from Steen's stick, hang heavy in his nostrils. Now the scents of the jungle came to him: heady smells of fringe grasses, indefinable scents of strange animals, and, underlying all else, the deep odour of damp leaves. He felt a sense of anticipation mingling with his fear.

The following day the same sunlight that poured gold onto the grasslands at the jungle's edge ran fingers of fire down his flanks, playing heavily on the black transverse stripes of his hide like a harp. Was that psychological? Because he knew that black absorbed the light while the red-gold between the bars reflected it? Possibly, but he liked the sensation even if it was mental rather than physical. He was beginning to become attuned to the new body, beginning to accept it for what it was. Marillac could never have imagined the pleasures of a cat before he had experienced them. They were more than sensual, they were sexual. The touch of the warm wind on the white belly-fur. The smell of musk thickening the air.

Being closer to the ground was an experience in itself. The hard-baked earth had its own beautiful smells, warm zones and traces of small creatures.

The jungle's border loomed before him, its black and impenetrable ribcage dripping with green and heaving like the flanks of some giant beast in the pulsing midday sun. He would not enjoy entering this living jungle. His jungle had been the steel corridors and compartments – the dangers of which walked on two legs and hunted in packs, the tunnel gangs.

He stayed on the fringe of the undergrowth that night, starting every few minutes or so at the sound of the lower orders of wildlife in the grass. While the human in him was afraid of the jungle's darkness and its unknown terrors, what constituted the tiger disliked being out in the open under a moonlit sky, and vulnerable.

When the morning came he tried to rationalise the two warring instincts inside him, and decided that the *tiger* had the least sensible of the two arguments, for a tiger's only enemy is Man – and Marillac at least had nothing to fear from that quarter. Nevertheless, he had to enter the jungle some time and it was better to do it in the light of day, fortified by a full stomach. Marillac pulled himself to his feet and padded towards the gate, and food.

They had lied to him.

Of course, now that he was thinking more clearly, now that the drugs had left his body, he could see that it would have been foolish to give him cooked meat. If he became reliant upon the handouts of food prepared for human consumption he might never leave the vicinity of the gate and hunt for himself. Hence he would not pass into that ribcage of trees except perhaps for water. That would not be 'living the life of a tiger in its own environment'.

Moreover, the raw meat left for him was still in the shape it had employed as a living thing: it was some kind of antelope – horns, hooves and warm skin. Warm? Marillac sniffed at the nostrils of the creature. It had not long been killed – perhaps a few minutes earlier. There was a neat hole burnt through its heart. He couldn't eat that, not a beautiful creature still retaining the ember-warmth of life. The whole idea was repugnant to him.

As he trotted towards the trees without having tasted the food, he realised that after two or three days there would probably be no meat of any kind by the gate. They would force him away from his last touch with civilisation, using his hunger as a spur. That Steen character, that smooth-talking bastard Steen, had manoeuvred Marillac into this ugly position. Clammy nightmares threatened him from outside, and he,

Marillac – timid little clown, cosseted throughout childhood because of ill health – was trapped within. There was no choice now. He began to panic and could feel that cat-heart pumping quickly beneath the fur. He was really trapped. He could throw that heavy-boned body at the gates and roar for all he was worth ... no one would come because *they knew* he had to eat, and to eat he had to find prey. He had to kill. They had him – Steen had him, just where he wanted him.

Marillac stopped at the edge of the trees and realised he was growling loudly. He pulled his mind back to his present situation with a jerk. It was tigerish, not human, to growl at the thought of revenge.

Close to, the trees were not as formidable as they had previously appeared and, with a preliminary cat-like sniff of the stifling air before him, he entered. It was dark inside, but more of a comforting darkness than a frightening one and he could smell water nearby. He would drink the water and then he would sleep. It was a very thick humid heat that enveloped his fur, damping it. He suddenly realised how tired he felt – during the hot day, not the night, was the time to fall asleep.

The leaves brushed against his glossy coat and he felt his powerful muscles gliding easily under the skin. He was power itself. Only the elephant could outmatch him for strength, and that was a huge clumsy beast, unworthy of even standing together with the tiger. Marillac was grace, was speed, was fierceness, was lashing, spitting, frightening power. Before he reached the pool he could hear the other animals scuttling away through the undergrowth. *They* were afraid of *him*? He growled with pleasure. No one had ever been afraid of Marillac before.

In the half-light he drank the brownish water, taking in weed and dead floating insects. As he drank he heard a noise above him. At first it was the sound of lizards running over waxy leaves, but it swiftly built up in volume until it was a thundering roar that made him begin growling again, until the drops eventually soaked through the thick foliage to further wet his fur and he realised what it was: a tropical rainstorm.

The rain lasted only an hour but during that time it was as intense as any waterfall. And afterwards the steam created such a heavy atmosphere that he fell into the sleep he desired, which lasted until nightfall.

That night he went back to the gate and ate the soft organs in the underside of the antelope, tearing open the gut and thrusting his face inside among the rank-smelling entrails. He hoped that Steen could not hear him. He felt he was debasing what was left of Marillac but the hunger had to be satisfied. To his surprise he did not vomit, and afterwards, with the gore still hanging from his spreading facial hairs, he made his way back to the jungle to clean himself, determined to put distance between himself and the gate through which he was sure Steen was spying on him.

~~~

Marillac had met Steen for the first time at university where they had both been lecturers – Marillac in the cartography of near-space and Steen in zoology. Both had an interest in the idea of adaptation to planetary or even local outside environments by exchanging the shell that housed the 'mortal coil'.

Transmutation experiments, animal to animal, had been carried out with a great deal of success, but they had that element of the unknown which made men recoil from any suggestion that humans might benefit from a reshuffling of their cell structure. People who had been moulded by their environment of enclosed cities were now the victims of their own protective measures: by isolating themselves from the elements they had made themselves dependent upon their own overcrowded but safe enclosures. They were weak, sickly, wan creatures for whom transmutation was a Godsend – if any of them dared to try it. People were not averse to changing bodies to save their lives, but they were afraid of losing 'themselves' as they were. They were afraid of 'dying' within another body.

Once it had been confirmed that Marillac was wasting away because of an unknown disease, which would relegate his body to a hoverchair or similar device, he resigned himself to the fact that he would have to change bodies, ready or not. They could use the cells that were not affected by the illness, the 'clean' cells, and multiply them. He had to pay for the treatment, however, by offering six months of his services to Steen's experiments. Steen, being a zoologist, was naturally fascinated by the idea of getting 'inside' an animal to learn of its ways, habits and fears. That he was too afraid to follow the desire through himself was plainly obvious, but what choice did Marillac have? Having no control over one's muscles meant an unpleasant life in which uncleanliness took over as a matter of course. The thought alone was repulsive to him.

2

The tiger came to a river that threw itself, like something hell-bent on destruction, down the glades and over molar rocks. Never before had Marillac seen anything so beautiful and it made him forget his hunger for a time. Green plants dipped spidery legs gingerly into pools, and others, like scalps, hung loosely over the waterfall washing their strands. A tall white bird fished with its sword-like beak in the waters below, treading warily among the rocks. It stabbed once, twice, and came out with a frog which disappeared in a flash down the sapling throat.

Marillac desperately needed food – he had eaten nothing for two days. Settling down below the waterfall, he allowed its thunder to lull him into a dream-like state while he kept his eyes open for signs of life. Sometime afterwards a frog leapt onto the bank and stared at the immobile tiger. He flattened it with a quick paw and gulped it down. Several more went the same way. Even a small once-feared snake met this unhappy fate.

Shortly after he had eaten, the Moon appeared over the trees and poured its cold light upon the jungle floor. There were men up there on that satellite, looking for useful minerals, building underground cities. Once he was back in the body of a man, Marillac hoped to join them, and those on Mars. In his mind he began to recite the names of the pioneers of Mars: Lecker, Spitzendon, Alverez; but after three he stopped, unable to remember the fourth or subsequent explorers. He had always known them before – as a child he could reel off the first thirteen names without even thinking. Perhaps that was the problem – he was thinking too hard. Lecker, Spitzendon, Alverez... Alverez... But what did it matter? He had far more important things to consider than the colonisation of the plants. (He *meant* 'planets'. Why did he think 'plants'?) Colonisation. Governments had vague ideas about colonizing the outer planets but were concerned with Man's physical ability to cope with the extreme conditions.

What if men were to change their bodies for those of animals? rumbled a theorist. Animals that *could* withstand the low temperatures, the varying pressures? Experiments with consenting humans (or parents' consent in the case of minors) were given the off-hand sanction and financial aid of the authorities. No one bothered to mention the other drawbacks: the lack of oxygenated atmosphere in which to work, the lack of food sources, the several other necessities of life which were not present on the planets. Why should they? It was another avenue of pure research, dear to people like Steen, that could be played with for several years before someone with common sense in a responsible position realised that money was being wasted.

A beetle crawled from beneath a leaf at his feet. He stared at it, curious to see what its mission was. The antennae waved and danced from its brow and its armoured legs picked cautiously at the ground beneath them. 'Are there beetles on other planets?' he wondered. He did not care for creatures like this, but all the same he was allowing it to pass over his paw for some distance before flicking it off. Perhaps the Moon was crawling with beetles? No, that was idiotic – there was no life native to the Moon. Then why did he see these black slow-limbed creatures picking their way across lunar webs – and why the visions of holes in the ground crawling with life? Men? 'They must be men,' he thought. Spidermen on the Moon. But even that seemed foolish and soon he dismissed the images from his mind.

That night, with his strength partially returned, he

swam the swift river and on the far bank had his first successful hunt. Breaking cover by the water's edge he came across a herd of wild pigs, and with his scent hidden in the billowing spray of the waterfall he brought down one of their young. He was surprised at how easy it was. Marillac held the kicking creature down with his weight and sank his teeth into the beast's bloated belly. It screamed shrilly, close to his ear, and he almost let it go in surprise; but after a while the noise stopped and he could feel warm blood running along his lip. Ravenous, he tore open the skin and fed on the warm meat. In the moonlight the animal's eyes glazed as death came up fast and finally overtook it.

~~~

The day was always hot. He blamed it for his fuzzy thinking and for the way his feverish mind ran amok with unreal scenes. Perhaps he did have a fever? Animals became sick just the way humans did. He was crossing the grassy plains, between the jungles, and game was abundant. But the sun was merciless as he searched for some shade under which to rest – his head pounded and every vestige of comfort left him when he could find no cool place under which to lie. No thorn bush – not even a single tree. He knew he was a Mongolian and he was only just shedding the last of his thick winter coat. Steen had not worried too much about species.

'Just a tiger,' he had said, when Marillac had had the temerity to broach the subject. 'Nothing special about it. A big one of course. Can't have you getting into a fight and coming out the loser, can we?'

Just a tiger, three feet tall at the shoulder and packed solid with muscle. A giant beast reaching fourteen feet in length. *Just* a tiger?

'Is a tiger very strong?' Marillac had asked.

'Strong? My God, there are some stories about tigers you just wouldn't believe. He's one of the most powerful of the land mammals.'

With these words Steen must have known he would strike home. A man as weak as a kitten, whose own muscles refused to answer the simplest of demands, would of course be impressed by strength.

'Even the pachyderms are afraid of tigers,' said Steen. 'They…'

The stories, old wives' tales stirred into a modicum of truth, fell on eager ears. Who would not want to be a lord for six months of his life, afraid of nothing, omnipotent among the beasts of the field? Certainly not a wasted man in Marillac's condition…

3

In the clearing were some stone ruins, covered in vines without and ulcerated by fungi within. There were some walls, almost hidden beneath grass and moss, and in the centre of the disturbed roughly hewn stones was an old temple, the eaves curling at the edges like dying leaves. Spiders' webs spanned the points of these eaves – the frail hands of ghosts.

The tiger made its way up the steps, littered with chips of quartz and twigs, and paused at the tall entrance. Inside it was black and smelled of a dynasty that patronised the night and gave gifts of men's lives to a dark god. Entering, it found the first stone altar, blood-black where once long knives sang and struck; the second supported a giant greenstone idol the height of three men. It sat cross-legged on the floor and had lightning cracks running through its torso. The upper limbs were outstretched to receive its blood-drenched offerings. These were stained and spotted with bird lime.

The three eyes were cold, hard and unreadable. They followed the tiger as it moved slowly around its base. Scratched on the block underneath, by some soldier of a foreign army, was the graffito: *Harris, 5th Infantry Brigade, The Jungle Bums.* No rank? thought Marillac. The writer must have been a conscript. All regulars were proud of their rank, whether private or general.

Marillac stared again at the face of the giant stone idol. The eyes regarded him steadily and made the fur rise on his back. The figure exuded a heavy air of malevolence, a wickedness that time had succeeded only in bringing to the surface of its shiny features. Its gaze was steeped in the knowledge of victimised children, struggling during the last throes of life. The high cheek-boned smile had grinned through a thousand attempts to sate its lust for the limbs of young women. And the glittering third eye, serving as navel in the overhanging belly, stared at its own gross parts.

Marillac's body was chilled to the heart. This was no god he knew of, no known religion. It filled him with dread. It was the god of some small dark age where men had lost themselves. An age during which they statued in fear at the sound of the temple gongs, and prayed that their god might go blind, or that some new benign presence would shatter it to fragments and take its place.

He left the halls quickly despite his fatigue, vowing never to return. Outside he found a new very real danger awaiting his exit from the temple's black interior. At the foot of the steps, head cocked to one side in a typical feline pose, was another tiger.

Marillac paused and steadied himself. This was something he had not bargained for. This was the materialisation of another of Steen's lies. Marillac was supposed to be the only tiger in the vicinity.

Now what did he do? The other half-shadow beast had risen to its feet and was regarding him steadfastly. It was definitely smaller than he was – a different variety. Its coat was a deep orange and black in contrast to the pale fuzzy markings that cut across Marillac. He could, he decided quickly, outrun this smaller beast if it became necessary. Perhaps, he thought wildly, the new tiger was another experiment? Another trapped man like himself, unable to tell him of his condition?

The tiger had covered three steps upward before Marillac growled involuntarily. The other stopped, seemingly puzzled. Would it know instinctively that he was a human in disguise? Would it smell his fear and know him for a man? *Would he have to kill this other animal in order to save himself?* My God, thought Marillac wildly, there's only one person I could kill right now, and that's Steen.

The smaller tiger began climbing again, cautiously. Marillac drew back his lips into a snarl and then gave out a hostile roar. Still it came until the man-tiger could smell the sweet odours to which his body, if not his mind, knew how to respond. There was to be no battle. Possibly a union, but no fight.

4

Some months later the two tigers reached the foot of the mountains and climbed up into the cooler air. The female was pregnant and the larger male, with the silver stud in its ear, wished to leave her in a place safe for the cubs before making a journey which he knew was inevitable.

They had had a good summer together, hunting and eating well; she had taught him the art of such livelihood. A small Sumatran, wearing her black-orange colours loudly, she would drive the game to him and he would make the kill. Once he had adjusted to a certain state of mind their teamwork became unbeatable, despite their mismatched camouflage. In the last jungle, set aside to cater for all the homeless animal species from all five continents, the wildlife was abundant.

His body suffered at times, from sores and chronic bladder complaints. Towards the latter she was silently sympathetic. But his sores were something she could actively doctor, by licking them clean for him where he could not reach himself.

It was a simple life, although in the early weeks he had thought he would go mad with boredom, but as time passed he found that hunting, resting, eating and caring for the other partner was a full existence with little time left for brooding. He found more and more that he had to think like a tiger to survive. She became angry when he made mistakes and chastised him with a sharpness that overrode his greater strength. He did not like that and pleasing her became his prime incentive in life. He slipped into an unreal state of mind. Unreal, that is, to Marillac's old way of thinking.

The mountains were not the place to spend the winter but they were remote and the need for protection was strong in both the tigers. He settled her in a spot where small game and tall grass was plentiful and eagles were scarce. There he left her.

The compulsion to retrace his wanderings was strong and there was a peculiar buzzing in his brain which he guessed was to do with the silver stud in his ear. She had tried to tear the thing out with her teeth but the pain had been too much and eventually he had pushed her away with a swing of his paw. It still hung onto the torn flesh of his ear. His mind and this thing were moving his legs, running them in the direction of the place from whence he had come. His heavy bulk trod lightly through the jungle on the springs that were his muscles, and the pads that were his feet. A face kept showing itself to his mind. There were other associated pictures which accompanied the face. He was vaguely aware that the man who owned that face had a name, but the buzzing in his mind would not now allow him to stop and consider what that name was. He pushed on, into the depths of the trees, towards the shouting river.

('...remember Marillac, if you become lost we can find you with the scanners. That stud in your ear not only identifies you to us, but also transmits a signal ... we shall be waiting for you at the time of the autumnal equinox, by the gate ... if not, we'll search for you so you won't be imprisoned within that body for ever. Just play the tiger ... we depend on you...')

He swam the river, narrower than before since no rain had fallen for some time and the spring snows had all gone from the mountains. Coming out on the far side he rested on the bank, drying his wet plastered coat until it fluffed shaggy again in the warm breezes. He dreamed the cat dreams of waterholes in the sun; of his female tiger turning in mock anger as he tried to mount her at the wrong time; of the electric ecstasy when it was the right time, and the warmth of her coat burned into his breast; of the buck brought down in full flight amid choking dust; of the horned mother driving towards his belly as he strove to make off with his kill. These were the dreams of a cat and there were none better.

The buzzing sounded again. He had forgotten it on hitting the cool water. It must have ceased its noise while he was swimming. Now it was like a hornet loose inside his skull, tormenting him, destroying his dreams. He lifted himself to his feet, the left hind leg giving him trouble where he had bruised it under the weight of that buck. He felt clean and fresh and strong, though. His tendons pulled at thick limbs that had never bent in servitude. His shoulders heaved at the head of a broad back that would carry no burden. He was the tiger, feared by all. Even the snakes and spiders which he had once loathed were to him a matter of indifference.

('…we want to know, at the end of it all, whether you have managed to adjust to your environment – whether you fit the role for which your body was designed. Above all, we want to know if, psychologically, you … well, frankly, if you're still sane … the stresses of such an experiment…')

He began his journey again. There was not much further to go. The edge of the jungle was only one day's walk.

('…you *will* be in your right mind of course. You're the ideal candidate for such … I mean, you've been imprisoned in a useless body for some time now. It'll be a release for you to be able to walk, run and roam at will – like a return to childhood…')

~~~

He broke out into the clearing at a run. It was past noon and the sun was behind him. Human scent had been strong for some time, rank in his nostrils; it quickened his heartbeat and he felt himself afraid. All his instincts rebelled against this meeting. They were men and he had been, was still, a tiger. He could see them waiting for him by the gate, their hands shielding their eyes. As he neared them he slowed to a trot, searching the faces. They had weapons. But the faces? One, no. Two, no. Three... Yes! The name finally flashed into his mind: *Steen*? He *had* remembered at the last moment.

Steen was smiling. Constructed thoughts struggled to the surface of the tiger's mind. The man was smiling because the experiment had been a success. They had done it together, the pair of them: two human minds and a tiger's body.

He slowed to an uneasy walk in front of them and they all began talking at once, laughing, gesturing and pointing at the silver stud in his ear. The movements were too quick, the sounds alien, and he hesitated, stepping backwards. The weapons of the men were lowered from their obvious positions, the owners seemingly embarrassed by their weight. They hung them down by their legs, almost out of sight behind their billowing clothes. And Steen was smiling, sweetstick between his teeth, nodding to his colleagues, each nod saying, 'I told you we'd make it – only the debriefing to go – matter of formality. Look at my tiger: sleek coat, muscled frame, bright eyes, strong jaws and sane as Sunday...'

The scent of the sweetstick wafted around Steen's head and was funnelled to the tiger by the wheeling breezes. It clogged his sensitive organs and red mist began clouding his confused brain. The already present adrenalin, making the blood surge through his veins, increased until the fear drummed panic in his ears and his nerves were taut with terror. Someone coughed sharply and Steen's hand jerked out, too fast. The net spread, a flimsy birdwing shape, above the tiger's head. The guns came up and hooks appeared in ready hands. It was clumsy. The net floated out and fell short. The gangling creatures were unskilled at capturing live beasts.

'Get him,' yelled Steen. An engine whined to life and a mechanical open-mouthed cage swept through the gates and descended upon the tiger.

The startled beast sprang from three yards away, jaws snapping at the narrow face. An object went spinning through the air like a smoking twig. The man went down, his spine snapping under the full weight of a mature tiger, his scream quenched by teeth that splintered the bones of his face and filled his throat with blood. The shock had killed him before the big cat tossed his body aside like a pet's toy.

Before the other men had recovered from the sudden attack the tiger was half-way back towards the jungle's edge. Then came the sound of thunder and the noise of hummingbirds caught in the tall dry grass. Just prior to entering the green darkness a stinging pain made him snap at his hindquarters. Then coolness closed over him, brushing his body as he made his way through it with rapid movements. The pain in his rear continued but it was bearable. Not a death wound, merely a heavy discomfort. He rested, breathing hard, the blood still racing.

Men would pursue him now. Hunt him down like a man-eater of old. They would come as noisy birds, and stoop like eagles out of the sun. They would come trundling like warthogs with their hands full of death – and they had their own ways to follow his spoor, to track him by his scent. The buzzing in his ear had already started again.

The first of the pursuers came into the jungle cautiously. The tiger hid, lying on his belly in the thick undergrowth. They passed on either side of him, having nothing with them yet with which to see through the leaves. He was tempted to attack when the offensive odour was all around and his sinews were tight with apprehension. When their smells had drifted away he began tearing at his ear with sharp claws, pulling, pulling, trying to scratch out the silver leech which drove him mad, now singing like a field full of crickets. Later it came free, with part of his ear, and he bit at it savagely for giving him so much pain, leaving teeth marks on its surface. His buttocks still hurt but the pain was dull and the blood had already stopped flowing.

On starting back towards the mountains he found the human trail was heading in the same direction and he felt the stirrings of fear within him for his mate. Humans hunting a tiger tend to be trigger-happy and do not stop to consider species or markings. They sight a tiger, possibly just the flash of a striped coat moving from rock to rock, and they make assumptions. They do not stop to make deductions when a man-eater is at large. They see, they kill – simply that. Some of them probably did not even know there was more than one type of tiger. They've seen one, they've seen them all, thought Marillac.

He thought about his unborn cubs and panic tightened his mind. There was enough of the old thinking left to know that he had to reach her before the humans did.

He travelled fast, not pausing for rest or food, and overtook them in a wide arc. They attacked in a noisy crowd as he was crossing the plain in front of them and came near to killing him this time. Only the high grasses saved him.

When they arrived at the foot of the mountains he let them know of his presence by walking through their camp at night, leaving his prints close to their beds. They had people watching all night but no one saw him enter or leave. Then he recrossed the plains in the dawn, treading along a soft stream bank to give them an easy path to follow. Then he waited, on the jungle's edge, to let them have a sighting.

Unknown to him, the foremost member of the group of the hunters was approaching from another angle; while he was offering only a slim target to the main group, his profile was presented to this man, whose weapon sang just as the tiger caught his scent. A hole was burned through the fleshy part of his throat and he span quickly for the trees.

5

When darkness came he limped his way towards the place of the tumbled-down stones, the temple with its smell of old deaths that had frightened him when he first became a tiger. It would be cool and dark inside,

The men came to the edge of the clearing just as he was climbing up the small even steps. Inside were two large blocks, one bearing the shape of a man in stone. He settled beside this one, facing the door. Soon the sounds and scents of men were all around and he growled softly in his own throat, feeling the now familiar tenseness building up within his strong body. Then there was a man, just a small distance away, standing at the entrance, peering in at him. The man-tiger kept very still, alert and ready to spring, his eyes on the man's eyes, waiting.

The man stared into the blackness of the room, his arm tipped with silver. The tiger could see the fear on the man's face, could smell it as it wafted into the enclosed space. There was no way of knowing if the man was frightened of finding a tiger in the dark or whether it was the place itself that was the source of the man's dread.

The buzzing began again in Marillac's head. This time there was no stud to blame – no irritant to scratch with his claw.

The sound was accompanied by a deep throbbing. Warped images slid into the room, from dark corners and recesses.

At the tiger's shoulder the criss-cross scratches of *Harris* began to dance; in the doorway was a new Harris, who would kiss the marble of God's cold lips. And God would suck the life from his body: God, the tiger and spirit of Marillac. Drugged with the old ways, what was once a weak man was now strong: Marillac – heady with the taste of Steen's blood.

He turned his huge head to look up at God. The stone chest was pulsing slowly, the old stone heart moving in time to the tiger's own.

His eyes went back to the figure in the doorway. Gradually the man entered, letting his arm fall down by his side. He trod softly over the slime-slick floors until he stood before God, mesmerised, as Marillac had been. The man was a thin, sickly creature – did they honestly think Marillac could go back to a body like that? Steen had known, but Steen was wise in the ways of men.

Above, the stone eyes glinted triumphantly and the cold lips were wet with pleasure.

No, not yet master, replied Marillac. *Let the others come to find him. Then, soon there will be more and more. Now that we have one, there will always be others. Men cannot leave a mystery unsolved.*

A heavy atmosphere descended, thick with the heat and the cloying scent of God's breath.

You know we will serve you well. You gave her to me. They are your spawn.

Then came the sound of running feet on the steps outside.

'Peterson? Are you up there?'

The eyes of the man in the room remained on the giant god's face.

'In here,' he called.

As the room filled with the stink of evil, Marillac's claws eased out of their sheaths. God smiled and began uncurling his own long thin fingers...

The Mountain
(A short tract about a tall giant)

There is a giant some call Chomolungma, and others Sagarmatha, to the north-east of Kathmandu, which swallows men and women whole. It eats them with its glacial jaws and leaves their brittle bones as human moraine, white on white, to sink beneath its ermine overcoat. It's a monstrous creature: cold, unfeeling, unbelievably hard, unforgiving of trespass. It draws its victims to their deaths simply by being there, by being the greatest and most formidable giant that ever existed. It has stood where it still stands for fifty-million years.

~~~

I am that giant. Immovable, rooted to the globe, but with a deep dark consciousness running through the veins, channels and galleries of my limestone being.

Conquer me if you dare, I say silently to the humans who come to stare and wonder. *I am here to be attempted by the fortunate brave and to destroy the unwary foolish. Some will reach my crest and rejoice. Yet even of those, the triumphant few, a handful will not touch the ground below again. Of the failures, a great many will not even reach my shoulders and yet will also die.*

Some have indeed stood on me, have been feted and now have their names etched in the annals of mankind's history. Others have sad tales to tell of feeble brains and lungs starved of breath; of slips and falls and broken bones; of lost extremities and rambling minds; of broken hearts and bitter mistakes. One of them once said, 'When I am sitting comfortably by my parlour fire, I want to be out there conquering the giant, but when I am there climbing the brute I want to be back by my parlour fire.' To defeat me is the ultimate challenge. There's never a year when there's not a horde, fully equipped and ready, determined to scale the great walls that are my shoulders, which have ripped the hopes of so many from their hearts. *I am the one*, each says to themself, *I am he or she who can subject this monster to my will.* They have not learned that I am untameable, that even if they reach the summit they will have nothing but awe in their hearts. Those who do not respect me, the arrogant and obdurate, will not walk away.

I am not an ogre with an ogre's ugly shape and face. My form is glittering, magnificent in its aspect. I shine blindingly in the sunlight. There are glimpses of my dark rocky shoulders, chest and back showing through a pure white apparel. I am not only the most savage, the most ferocious giant in the world, I am the most beautiful. My features are manifold: arete bridges, fathomless chasms, glaciers laced with seracs, strident peaks and spires, deep soft valleys, wind-honed ridges wearing spindrift veils, crystal cliffs and throated gullies. I am too massive and unyielding to love; too remote and alien to touch any heart. You can admire, you are stupefied, you are overcome with emotion when confronted with my presence, there is veneration. To some I am a deeply hallowed being, a holy entity. Others find spiritual fortitude when they stand before me. I strike men and women dumb with reverence. Other lifeforms know me better than humans do and walk my ways with infinite care. My heights defy all creatures but the crane, goose and chough. Even the eagle does not dare.

Other giants wear clouds for shawls, but none so often as me. The swirling mists and blinding blizzards that wrap themselves around my form come time and again without warning. One moment the king of the massif is here, the next gone. I come and go and am usually longer in the going. An occulting spectre. In my hidden form I am deadly. Those on my slopes may vanish in the vapours, never to be seen again. With the spalling of my coat of ice, the shedding of my cloak of snow, they tumble to their ends. Some are crushed under the weight of my vestments; others are swept into crevices and chasms. I am, it is true, unfeeling, merciless, apathetic. Not just a heart of stone but mineral through and through. I own the wind and the sky, the cold and the sun, the peace and the stillness. I kill without meaning. I care nought for the suffering.

I am older than death itself.

The World's Smallest Giant

Jill's father was very poor, having lost all his money betting on the horses and cards. He was a gambler and didn't trust himself with the last few thousand pounds in his savings. So he gave them to his daughter and said, 'Use this to invest on the stock market. Perhaps we'll get lucky and make a fortune.'

Jill went online and started to look for a reliable financial firm with which to invest the family money on the stock market. However, on the way she came across an advertisement, as one invariably does when trawling the internet. It said:

Organic Building Bricks!
They grow into amazing edifices!
Buy five of these fantastic bricks and
grow yourself a mansion!'

She was impressed by the number of exclamation marks in the advert and thought, this product must be genuine with such striking punctuation! There was a picture of a beautiful house with gardens and a swimming pool and peacocks wandering round the grounds. It looked idyllic and Jill was entranced. However, though she was a practical girl, when it came to making plans she was a little dreamy about what to do with the money.

She thought: 'If we buy some of these bricks we can grow a block of flats in the middle of the city and let them at reasonable rents. We probably won't become rich but father and I will be able to live comfortably for the rest of our lives.'

So, she purchased the five organic bricks advertised on eBay, the last of the stock, so the advert said, and waited impatiently for the postman. When they arrived they looked quite ordinary and the postman had been a bit grumpy because the parcel was very heavy. Delighted with her purchase she went to her father and told him what she had done. He looked at her aghast and then began to shout at his daughter, calling her the most foolish child her mother had presented him with. He took the bricks and threw them out of the window, then stomped out of the house to find a penny-ante card game.

Jill went to bed feeling very miserable, but the next morning she was amazed to find a skyscraper in their back garden. Delighted, she went in. It appeared to be all ready for tenants, both residential and office space. She took the lift to the top where she found the penthouse already occupied. She rang the bell and a man answered the door. He was small, bald and with a weaselly-looking face.

'Can I help you?' he said in a gruff voice. 'I'm rather busy at the moment making lots of money.'

Jill replied, 'I'm the owner of this building and I'm wondering how you managed to get in?'

His manner changed abruptly and he explained that he was someone who slept very little and had been wandering the streets in the early hours, thinking about things like the kick he got out of sacking staff and breaking up conglomerates using company leverage. 'The door was unlocked when I arrived, so I let myself in, and am impressed. I'm a Giant-of-Industry,' he explained. 'You must have heard of me. Martin Manduck? I'd like to rent this apartment from you. Name your price.'

'Well,' Jill replied, 'I haven't actually looked at it myself yet but if you allow me to come in and assess what it's worth I'll give you a fair rental figure.'

Manduck agreed and Jill entered to find the place fully furnished with the most luxurious sofas, beds and carpets. In one corner was a strange looking device. She asked what it was. 'Oh that,' he replied. 'It's a unique machine that mines bitcoins. It's what started me off and keeps me going when I make bad investments and lose all my money.'

'Does that happen often?'

'Oh, quite often. I'm used to it now. It's part of the process so of being an entrepreneur. You make a huge fortune, you go bust, you filch the pension fund, you lose that too, you file for bankruptcy, and then you start again. This is my starter kit.'

The Giant-of-Industry went to fetch his cheque book while Jill stared at the unique machine. It was a tangle of wires with a golden ball at its heart. She decided it resembled a large bird with a long neck. What a fabulous device to have, though! She had heard of bitcoins, and they seemed to soar in value by the day. Yes, rentals would keep bread on the table but an item like this could make one rich. And she had heard of Martin Manduck too. He owned all the newspapers in the country and had governments in his pocket. He paid his workers miserable wages and was known to be ruthless with competitors. Indeed, he was not regarded as being an asset to the nation and was generally held in contempt for his business practices. There had been a partner who was now destitute and roaming the streets with no soles to his shoes.

~~~

Jill formed a plan. She watched the exit to the skyscraper from the window of her house that faced her garden. When she saw Manduck come out the building she went in. She took the lift to the penthouse. Being the landlord she had key to the apartment. She let herself in and straight away grabbed the unique machine that looked like a large domestic bird. However, as she was about to leave Manduck returned. He witnessed her in the act of stealing his property, gave a yell and tried to grab her. Jill was young and nimble and managed to duck under his outstretched right arm.

She ran to the lift and took it to the ground floor, whereupon it shot up again, presumably at the command of Martin Manduck. She went immediately to the control box on the wall in the entrance and opened the door. When the lift started coming down again, she reached in and ripped out a nest of wires: red, green, blue, yellow. There was a horrible clunk from somewhere high in the building, then the sound of whooshing accompanied by a terrible screaming. The screaming came to an abrupt end when the lift smashed to pieces down below her feet in the underground car park. Jill waited a minute or two then called for an ambulance. When it arrived they in turn called the mortuary.

Jill and her father became very wealthy and were regarded in the city as prodigious philanthropists who never turned away a worthy cause.

~~~

This is a fairy story. Fairy stories are often cruel and the heroes get away with theft and murder. Look at 'Hansel and Gretel'. Look at 'Vasilisa the Beautiful'. Jill is not pursued by the law because there are no police

forces in fairy tales. Everyone lives happily ever after;
all those left alive, that is.

The Ice Giant

High up in the polar regions a dark mass formed. Although no thicker and no more viscous than a shadow, it had sentience. Where it came from originally, Kallik never discovered. Nor why it came to be or how it came to be. It had no real substance, being something in the way of a slice of dark wind. It had been created during that long-winter North Canadian night, so perhaps it was simply a cankerous scab of evil, a malignant blight that had gathered on the general body of the blanket of the sunless northern regions.

Kallik didn't concern himself with the why or wherefores too much. It was enough for him to know that this thing had at its core a malevolent spirit, a nature bent on the destruction of natural living creatures. By the time it came to his attention, this amorphous entity had gathered ice around itself, protecting its vulnerability with a suit of armour. The entity itself was merely the heart of a huge figure with the rough contours of a human being. Kallik suspected that its giant shape had been copied from the first man it had killed, quartered, and distributed over the snowy landscape of the polar wastes.

At first, finding the frozen dismembered parts of one of his neighbours, Kallik had thought the culprit might be a bear, though they were hibernating at this time of year. On inspecting the remains though, there were no signs of claw or fang marks. Yet something, a creature of some kind, had ripped this man apart. It was not another human. The limbs had not been severed with a tool; they had been gripped and pulled out of their sockets. So, Kallik's reasoning, having gone through the plausible and known, naturally drifted into the mythological and legendary, using the less credible mindset of his ancestors.

His grandfather had told him there was once a race of giants which had inhabited the northern regions. They were called the Tuniit. Was it possible that one of these creatures, a giant, had committed the murder? However, even Kallik's grandfather had never actually seen one of the Tuniit, which were now believed to be extinct. What about the Ijiraq? These were shape-changers, bent on evil simply for evil's sake. Indeed, Tuniit were only interested in sucking out the strength of a man or woman through an iron pipe. They would not have bothered to rip a flaccid body apart and scatter it over the tundra.

No, he told himself, he had here something quite different. Had it been one of the Tuniit he might even have been comforted to know that these ancient beings had not disappeared from the world. It would be evidence that perhaps life was not all machines and devices, as it seemed to be now; that there were natural mysteries still to be solved. This monster was not in any way or form a natural being. It was from the paranormal, from the other side of the aurora curtain that divided the familiar from the strange and menacing.

Kallik's occupation was not traditional. He was an Inuit. Though one or two of the younger generation had left the old ways and gone south, Kallik had never even considered doing so; he had taken up with work that his grandfathers did not do. Unlike them he was a herdsman with a number of reindeer; these had been introduced into Northern Canada from Siberia in the early part of the century. Kallik's friends and neighbours were amused by his love of the reindeer and stuck to the older tradition of ice fishing and seal hunting, to keep themselves warm and fed in their harsh environment. In the winter he lived in igloos, one near his heard and another where his wife and children stayed. When he was able to leave his herd he returned to his more permanent home. Thus, he lived a semi-nomadic existence on the tundra.

~~~

The nightmare began when one of his reindeer became lost in a snowstorm and he went out in search of it on his snowmobile. When he found it, the animal's head had been torn off. It had been thrown far from the cadaver. It was on his way back to his igloo that he found the leg of a man, then after a further search, an arm and a head. He could do nothing for the human victim, though he knew he would have to report it to the authorities; but before he did that he intended to seek the perpetrator of the crime against his reindeer. The thing that had done these two foul deeds was a monstrous killer and in Kallik's world you dispensed justice yourself, swiftly, before allowing the authorities to spend an eternity trying to do the same thing inefficiently and incompetently.

The day after his return, Kallik packed his gear – provisions, rifle, ammunition, fuel – and set off on his snowmobile northwards. Overhead, the light from the stars was cutting through the blackness and then lower down becoming dimmed by the beam from his machine. It was minus-seventeen Celsius and even though he was used to the cold, having been born and bred to it, he felt the chill on this night. The sound of his engine seemed louder than normal, but the cold and the noise were probably bothersome only because his heart was racing, and he was feeling a mixture of fear and excitement. On the fear scale, it had not gone into the terror zone but remained in that area where extra caution and alertness was necessary. He did not want to be surprised by something coming at him out of the darkness.

Kallik returned to the place where he'd found the human body parts. There'd been a light fall of snow but not enough to cover the deep tracks left by the killer. They were huge. This spoor went through a forest of spruce and fir trees covered in pure white snow which dazzled in the machine's headlight. The trees were ghostly sculptures, some of them thin and needle-like, others with overcoats of whitened fir. There was a wind, but not high enough to shake the snow from the trees. Kallik navigated through the forest with ease, being as comfortable in the saddle of his mobile as a Mongolian horseman on his stocky mount.

After two hours he broke through the forest and was on an open glacier plain. He swiftly cut the engine of his machine and stared into a misty haze of light snowflakes, with a backlit curtain of aurora filling the sky. He could see a shape in the distance, a huge figure of a man. A white colossus, its exact form was blurred by the poor visibility. Kallik left his snowmobile where it was, took his rifle, and proceeded on snowshoes towards this giant statue.

The thick legs of the thing were wide apart and its arms were in an upturned V away from the torso. It was immense, standing around ten metres high. The closer he came to it the clearer it became. When he was half-a-kilometre away he saw it move. A spike of fear went through Kallik's body. *What's this? Was the thing alive, or was it some kind of machine?*

Kallik naturally halted his progress at this point, wondering what to do. If this giant was responsible for killing his reindeer and the unknown corpse, it would be stupid to advance. It would take more than a rifle bullet to stop such a monster. Better to retreat now and gather his thoughts, form some sort of battle plan. Perhaps he could lure it over a cliff or into the sea? Certainly, it was foolish just to go charging in and hoping for a miracle.

The giant began to step out now. It had obviously become aware of the intruder. Whether it had seen, sensed, or gathered this awareness intuitively, Kallik did not know or care. The giant looked as if it were made of pure ice, and it was stepping with authority and determination.

Kallik turned and hurried away as fast as his snowshoes would allow. He had that half-a-kilometre start on the being and he was going to need it. Thick clothes and snowshoes were cumbersome items for a runner on the white ground which lay between him and his vehicle. Still, he was a fit man, in his prime, and he knew, judging by the speed of his pursuer, that he could outdistance the giant once on his snowmobile.

Indeed, he got to his machine a football field ahead of the thing that was bearing down on him. Once in the saddle he unslung his rifle and levelled it at the great head of ice. The face was blank of any expression and the eyes looked like milky balls without lids or pupils, but Kallik took aim at one of them. The rifle kicked at his shoulder and the sound of the shot filled the hollow of the night. The ice giant's head jerked back and something flew from the right side of its skull. The round had gone through the eye and had exited around where an ear would have been, if the monster had ears. There was a large hole now where the shot had come out and taken a chunk of ice with it.

Kallik started the engine of his machine and spurted through the snow into the forest. He slalomed in and out of trees which he hoped would reduce the giant's progress. They did. The monster tried crashing through them in a straight line, but this only served to slow it down. Then it tried to weave between them, but it was a heavy and cumbersome. Before long it fell well behind the quicker snowmobile. Kallik kept going until he reached what he considered to be a safe distance and paused. He knew now that he could outrun his opponent, which was a great boost to his confidence.

The herdsman now had to decide what to do about this monstrous ice giant. He could wait until the warmer weather came and then it would melt, but only if it stayed as far south as it was now. However, it might head north, up into the Artic, and survive the summer months. In the meantime his people would be subject to violence and terror from this malformed creature.

Killak decided it was time to bring in some of his friends and relatives. He set off to the nearest community.

~~~

Indeed, from that day on, the ice giant began to ravage the tundra, slaughtering and maiming and killing one family of Inuit as they were travelling from their home to another community. There was no real motive behind the destruction and death. The ice giant didn't eat the people it killed, nor use them as bait for some other prey. It seemed simply a case of evil incarnate. There was something inside it that was driving this monster: a demon of some kind that had awakened and formed a body of ice around itself. A rampant iceberg on the wastes, it was smashing the wilderness to pieces, even roaming deep down into Saskatchewan and lower down still. The Inuit hoped it would stay there, but of course it returned well ahead of the warmer weather.

A demon, on its own, made of nothing but darkness, could do nothing physically, but now that it was a solid entity it was able to run ruthlessly wild amongst mortals. It probably thought itself clever and invincible in its glacial form. They could hear it coming when it ran riot: the cracking of its joints, the crashing of its feet on the permafrost ground. When it stamped over a frozen lake its feet drummed up a thunder that frightened all living creatures. No sound came from it, unless it was that of timber being smashed to splinters by its fists, or the terrible cry of pain from a living creature in its grip.

The horrifying thing to those who were used to the stillness, the peaceful nature of their snowy domain, was that this demon knew how to strike unease in a human heart. Had the demon chosen to present itself as an animal of some kind, even a bear, they could have fought it as men fight rogue beasts. Instead, it had cunningly decided to copy the human figure, the shape and contours of a man, which terrified the young and filled the old with anxiety

We do not like distorted images of ourselves –

phantoms, skeletons, masks, ugly statues – which fill us with a particular dread of dark malevolence within ourselves. Evil manifest, the Devil and his kind walking the Earth is so abhorrent to us we try to ward it off with holy signs, symbols, chants, rituals and prayers. We know they probably do not work, yet we appease our untameable naked fear with these useless weapons we have invented to fight a supernatural foe.

The Inuit fought it with their rifles, but these weapons were puny against such a monster. However, a fisherman, surprised at his ice hole, managed to take off the nose of this effigy of human form. He found the nose lodged in the branches of a spruce the next day and took it to show Kallik. The herdsman had already formed a suspicion in his mind and this lump of ice confirmed it.

'You are sure this comes from the giant?' he asked.

'I am. It was my bullet that took it from its face.'

It was coming on early Spring. The giant would soon be moving north to keep itself within freezing temperatures. However, Kallik was aware of something that the demon inside the ice giant seemed not to know, so he drew up a plan to defeat this being. In order for it to work, he and his friends and relatives had to lure the giant to where they wanted it to be. In order to do this they broke the ice on a lake and used it to build a magnificent giant of their own.

There were ice sculptors amongst them and the finished statue, easily as large as the rogue ice giant that plagued them, was beautiful to view. It had a wreath of ice leaves around its head, regular handsome features on its face with eyes of blue ice, a muscled body with well-proportioned limbs, and a strong aggressive-looking stance. The people were very pleased with it, but of course the rogue ice giant was not. It saw the new giant as a physical challenge, found it arrogant in the extreme and was very jealous of its good looks. It had to move south to fight the upstart intruder, but the newcomer was frozen solid, so it had no fear of being led into an area with a dangerous temperature.

So the killer set off southwards towards its enemy. Crashing through the forests it came, its attention fixed on destroying that parvenu who had dared to invade its territory. It took several days before the new giant approached, despite that both were so tall they could be seen for many miles over the flat snowy landscape. In the daylight the newcomer shone maddingly, translucently, as if it were some kind of beautiful prince among ice giants. This of course incensed the aggressor further. All the attacking giant wanted to do was to punch that smirk off its conceited face and smash its crystal form into icicles. Almost mindlessly, it continued to bear down on its opponent, sure in the knowledge that it was the heavier and most powerful of the two entities.

The nearer it came to do battle, however, the slower it became. Suddenly this killer of beasts and men realised it was melting. It did not understand how this could be, when the other ice giant looked as freshly frozen as if it was in the most comfortable of temperatures for its kind. At first it paid no heed, thinking it was probably because it was moving rapidly over the landscape that its body had begun to shed water; it decided that friction was causing the melting and that would stop once it had broken its adversary to pieces and then started on that crowd of mortals who were watching. Did they think their champion was going to triumph? How stupid were these humans!

Yet the thaw did not stop and before long it had been drawn so far south it could not escape. It did indeed finally reach its smug detested target, destroying it with several punches and kicks. Then it had to set off from whence it had come, its armour melting, water running from it in rivulets, now ignoring the humans.

The men and women it had terrorised over the winter months followed, stalking the foul thing that had made their lives a misery. Northwards it went to get into those regions that never went above zero, but the temperature had started rising when it had set out for the south and the demon within it knew it could not reach safety. It could see amongst the humans who tagged along behind that there was a shaman among them. Once its armour had gone and it was exposed to the world, the demon would be vulnerable. Annihilation was close.

Finally, in its frustration and anger, the dark entity turned and tried to take the clusters of men with it to its end. However, its carapace was now quite thin and fragile. The followers beat it with hunting spears until its shell lay in shards on the ground. The shadow tried to escape, of course, tried to reach some deep dark forbidden place before it could be obliterated by the spells of the shaman.

It was a hopeless and pitiful attempt.

Those cunning creatures called mortals had defeated it.

~~~

On my next visit to the Artic Circle, and on being told the story of the battle, I sought out the giant killer

Kallik. I asked him how it was that his giant statue had remained frozen while the rogue giant had melted.

'Ah,' he said, smiling pleasantly at my ignorance, 'you see, when we had the nose that had been knocked off our enemy's face, I licked it. Sure enough, there was a faint taste of salt.'

He paused for effect then added, 'Our giant had been carved from freshwater ice, from a lake The demon was made of seawater.'

'Right,' I said, nodding at his resourcefulness, 'sea ice melts at a lower temperature than fresh ice. You tricked him to come too far south.'

'We never call such things *him* or *he*,' replied the Kallik, 'always *it*.'

Rübezahl

I was born a teacher in the year 1776. I think I taught my innumerate and illiterate Bohemian parents to count while still an infant. I couldn't speak of course, not yet having learned how, but I held up fingers for the number of things I wanted. One, I wanted to pee. Two, I wanted to do something more substantial. Three, I wanted a drink. Four, I wanted that many spoonfuls of malt (I did love malt). Five, I wanted to go to sleep. And so on and so forth. After a year we got to the toes and not long after that I learned to talk and was able to teach them properly. After I myself learned to read and write, almost by instinct, I taught my beloved parents to enjoy the ripest fruits of literature.

They told everyone I, Franz Kopke, was bound for prince-hood, but of course that never came to pass. Instead, I became Professor of Literature, Mathematics and Languages at Heidelberg University. However, those three disciplines are quite limiting, and it follows that when you can actually read a book there are no academic or even practical subjects that remain beyond your understanding. My renown as a teacher spread through the whole world and although I never became a prince, I taught many of them and their sisters, and at one time even the Pope invited me to the Vatican in order to explain the ontology of scripture in the ethics of interpretation in the theology of several different priests ranging over a dozen individual centuries.

However, this is a story, a true one nonetheless, and I must try not to get too erudite or sesquipedalian (there, I've done it again!) in my usage of words.

~~~

I heard by way of mouth that Rübezahl, the great giant who lives in the Krkonoše Mountains, wanted me to come to him. The message was passed on by one of the lesser giants who were his contact with the lower world. Now Rübezahl had at one time been a shape-changer and in that era he might well have visited me in person as an elf or an owl – a creature able to get about in the normal way. For a giant of his size, of course, it would have been catastrophic for him to come down to us ordinary mortals. The accidental damage he might have caused was unthinkable.

Anyway, the message reached me and I had to think hard about it. If I went I would be neglecting my students. I also had papers to write on various themes and subjects in order to keep my reputation and that of the university in vogue. If one lapses for even a short period the upstart professors of lesser academic institutions refuse to be kept at bay. Those jackanapes begin to believe they can build a status beyond their scholastic ability and can rival the old, established universities: that of Oxford, Padua, Cairo, Salamanca, and of course Heidelberg, to name but five that spring to mind. However, I gave it some considerable thought by candlelight through a long and quiet night, coming to the conclusion that if the giant wanted me, it was for my academic muscle. Satisfying the giant's thirst for knowledge could well enhance my career and the prestige of the university. I sought permission from the Chancellor to go and it was granted.

I gathered together a knapsack of books on various

subjects: Euler's *Methodus inveniendi lineas curvas maximi proprietate gaudentes,* Newton's *Philosophiae Naturalis Principia Mathematica,* Galileo's *Dialogue Concerning the Two Chief World's Systems,* and one or two other important works, along with paper and writing equipment. Rübezahl had not indicated what he wished to learn, what questions he had for me, what revelations were expected from me. I was feeling in the dark but I hoped I had chosen those works which would assist me in my endeavours to help the giant to an understanding, be it in natural philosophy, mathematics, world politics, theology, or some other branch of knowledge.

Once I was ready I set off first by coach, then on horseback and finally on foot. I found a guide called Petr in the small foothill town of Spindlermühle. Petr was a sturdy-legged intelligent man of some standing in his town, having rescued many a lost traveller from the dark forbidding massif that loured over the border between Bohemia and Silesia. Rübezahl lived on the highest of the Bohemian peaks: Sněžka at some 1,600 metres. I had never been higher than the third storey bedroom in my Heidelberg lodgings. I was full of trepidation in my endeavour to scale the fastnesses of this mountain range.

'I will look after you as if you were my own father,' said the calming Petr. 'Please, just rely on me and do everything I say. I am very used to looking after those who wish to explore my back yard.'

The 'back yard' proved to be the most physical challenge of my life. Petr went slowly and cautiously enough for me, but I am unused to climbing anything more demanding than a staircase. The foothills took my breath and rammed it back down my throat, so when we came to real mountain climbing I was both terrified and exhausted. Still, Petr made sure I was securely roped to him, which was kind because if I fell I would surely have taken him with me. He also carried my belongings including the weighty books. We scaled steep inclines and rested on ledges when I could go no further at that moment.

Once, we saw one of the lesser giants swinging from crag to crag like an orangutan. He was very hairy and quite naked, and muscular, so he could well have passed for a jungle creature except for his expression, which changed from one of curiosity to one of annoyance. Petr called to the fellow but got no verbal response. The giant – he was, in my estimation, about four metres in height – disappeared around a chimney and we saw nothing of him after that. Petr told me the fellow would go back and inform his tribe of intruders.

'Will they attack us?' I asked. 'Perhaps we should arm ourselves with some clubs?'

He laughed. 'No, they won't harm us, not physically. They might come and jeer at us in their own language, but why should that worry us? We won't even understand the insults. Now, come, we must get on. We don't want to find ourselves in a dangerous place at nightfall. At least there's no snow at the moment, but it will be very cold. We need to settle in some hollow or below an overhanging rock. You did well to bring a good thick coat with you.'

'Well, Rübezahl will give me a bed, will he not? Once we get to his cabin?'

Again, the laugh. 'Bless you, he doesn't have a cabin. He has a cave and there's no bed in there, only a dirt floor. Caves can be quite warm though. They keep the same temperature however hot or cold it is outside.

He'll probably give you some bear hides as blankets. They may be a bit smelly, since he isn't too fussed about curing them properly, but you won't freeze to death under his roof.'

That night we found a sort of corner in the rockface away from the wind and I tried to sleep, but I managed only to doze fitfully. I was wondering why I had let myself in for this adventure, which was beginning to take its toll on my nerves and my body. What was I thinking of? I thought. I was no mountaineer and I had never spent a single night outside a bed with sheets and blankets. I was almost on the point of asking Petr if we could turn round and go back down to the safety of civilisation. However, when I hinted at it, he told me that we were not far from our destination and to gather my courage and force myself onward, up this rock fortress, home of the lesser and greater Bohemian giants.

~~~

We saw Rübezahl from a long way off. He was three times the size of that lesser giant we had seen. When he saw us coming he sat down and studied us as we walked towards him. Petr stopped some twenty metres away from him and nudged me forward. 'Go ahead,' he murmured, 'this is your expedition.'

Nervously, I approached this huge creature, the top of his head and brow momentarily obscured by a passing cloud. Unlike his cousins he had very little hair on his body, but the pitch-black hair on his head flowed over his shoulders and down his body. When he was standing it touched the ground. I was amazed by the silken look of it, as if it had been washed and oiled for his visitors, while the rest of him was quite grubby. His head was enormous and out of proportion to the rest of his frame. His features were pleasant enough, or would have been on a man my size, all except the nose which jutted out like a dark upturned boat. The feet too were huge and out of proportion, but the hands had slim heavily calloused fingers that looked quite feminine. The sort of fingers that a would-be musician might yearn for when learning to play the lyre. What also struck me as I approached was that his eyelashes were so sweeping and long they looked like blackbirds fluttering their wings when he blinked.

'Sir,' I began, though it hurt my neck to look up into his face. 'I have come at your behest to pass on knowledge.'

I always avoid the word 'teach' because it sounds patronizing, especially in the Slavic tongue I had heard he used.

He nodded slowly. 'You are the wise professor?'

'I am the professor and some call me wise, but I would not myself claim to deserve that epithet.'

I began to lay out my books on the ground in front of him and saw that he had bent his head to look at them.

'Are you able to see the titles?' I asked. 'Which would you prefer to start with?'

'What are they?'

I was somewhat startled and immediately my heart sank.

'Why, books of course.'

'With writing in them?'

'Writing and illustrations.'

'Let me see.'

I opened the *Methodus* at a random page and said, 'You will not be able to understand the language, but I will explain as we go along.'

He poked at the page with a long dirty finger.

'This is writing?'

My heart sank further.

'Yes, writing,' I replied, my voice almost lost in the back of my throat.

'Good.' His voice became deep, rich and warm, not overpowering in volume. 'You must teach me this writing.'

'You – you want to learn to read and write?'

'I am an ignorant person.'

My hope for wide academic fame from this meeting was fading rapidly. They would be laughing at me, my rivals.

So, you taught a fool how to write? I could hear them cackling. *Which village schoolmistress isn't able to do the same?*

An eagle flew near to Rübezahl's head and he swatted at it as if it were an insect, but fortunately for the bird he missed.

I gathered my wits. 'But not so ignorant as to fail to realise the worth of learning. Tell me, why do you *want* to know how to read and write?'

'Not to read. Just to write.'

'Unfortunately, the two go together. You can't do one without the other. First you must learn to read, then you need to...'

'If I must, then I must. Can we start? I will die very soon now, and I wish to write the story of my life so that others may know I was here on the mountain. I do not want to die and there be nothing left to say that I lived.'

'You – you want to write your memoirs?

'Is that what it is, a memoir? I don't know this word.'

I tried for an escape. 'You could tell me your story and I could write it down for you.'

He shook his massive head and his cascading hair shimmered in the light.

'That would not be right. It would not be my voice.'

'Well, it would be your words.'

'Perhaps not.'

And he stared hard and long at me with a look I knew well. Suspicious princes and prelates had given me such a look while I was translating their words into a foreign language. It said, *How do I know you are passing on exactly what I say? You could be making me look like an idiot.*

Petr, still standing way back had heard the whole of this exchange and he laughed and shouted, 'Got your work cut out, eh professor?'

I turned angrily on him. 'Please keep your opinions to yourself. If this – this person – wants to learn to write, I am the man to teach him. I should have guessed but I doubt any of his kind has ever done the same. When I leave him he will be able to trot out his autobiography, no doubt the first written record of a giant's life to enter the libraries of the world. You are looking at an academic whose fame is assured, my friend. You would be wise not to scoff.' I spoke with fervour and determination but inside did not feel as confident as I hoped to appear to Petr.

'Oh, I wasn't scoffing, sir. Please believe me. I pray you might be successful – I am just a little doubtful of your student's ability.'

Fortunately, Rübezahl did not seem to take offence at this remark.

Shortly after this Petr left, back down to the valley.

~~~

Thus began my time in the mountains and an interesting but strange period it was. Rübezahl was an indifferent host. When my attempts at teaching him to read were not in session he left me to my own devices. If I wanted anything I had to ask for it because it would not be offered. Every single meal was prefaced with me saying, 'Isn't it time to eat? May I join you?' If I said nothing he would cook only for himself, usually the carcass of a wild boar or some kind of deer, brought up to him by one of the lesser giants who seemed to stock his larder weekly. Whether they did it out of good neighbourliness or fear of a greater being I do not know. They also brought greens and the odd few loaves of bread, but meat was always on the menu.

When I requested something for myself I would be tossed a chunk of venison or boar which had been charred on an open fire. He usually let me share any bread that he had. I became used to, even fond, of burnt meat dripping with hot fat, which ran down the corners of my mouth. I knew my body would not stand such fare forever, of course, and that was another thing that worried me.

He could not seem to hold any knowledge in his head for more than a day. I would patiently teach him the alphabet in the morning, he would recite it in the afternoon quite clearly and accurately, but by the next morning his mind was a blank. Sleep seemed to wipe his mind clear of new knowledge. I would have to begin all over again, trying to hammer the letters into his brain. It was an exhausting business and I despaired of him even getting over that first stage of learning to read and write. Memoirs? A hopeless task. A swirling dream.

I would go to bed at night on my bearskins, praying

that something would stick in his head, even if only those first three letters: ABC.

~~~

The cave was not an unpleasant place to call home. It was actually a series of caverns, one of them with a ceiling so high I could not see the stalactites. The place was a diamond mine of Arachnida, insects, bats and the occasional reptile, which kept me busy, when I was not teaching, classifying fauna. Busy indeed, for not many people realise that there are around 45,000 species of spiders alone in the world, and so the study of such invertebrates is endlessly rich.

Occasionally, a predacious beast would wander into the camp: a bear, a lynx, a wolf, something of that sort. They did not usually stay long with the smell of giant in the air. Then winter came and I was cold much of the time. One night a bear wandered in, probably looking for a warm place to hibernate. I slept close to the entrance of the first cavern for one reason only: Rübezahl's huge farts were deadly. He slept in the large third cavern, so I kept as far away from him as possible. (Once we found a fox that had crept into the second cavern during the dark hours and had been asphyxiated). Anyway, the bear started to cause a fuss when it saw me. The noise woke Rübezahl who came up out of the depths and simply picked up the poor beast and threw it out into the night.

Sometimes there was a heavy mist on the mountain but most mornings we woke to clean clear air which was beneficial to my lungs. It was probably one of the best years of my life. Physically and mentally, I was in my prime. There were no petty worries to concern me: no bills to pay, politics to ponder, or small aggravating battles with colleagues. I was able to write and draw freely and easily, which had the giant looking over my shoulder in wonder. We got on well enough together too. It was not like being closeted with another human being with all the unpleasant personal traits we as a race employ. He kept to himself outside lessons and I could wander off and explore our surroundings if life became too claustrophobic.

The lessons were tortuous and torturous however, with my trying to bore the tiniest piece of knowledge into a skull thick as that of a giant tortoise's shell.

'You understand the letters of the alphabet have a sequence?' I said. 'Once you learn the rhythm you will be able to trot them out with ease.'

'What is this *sequence*? I do not know this word.'

'Well, it's like when you count. One, two, three, four, five ... the figures come in set order, don't they?'

'I do not count with my mouth; I hold up fingers to show how many.'

'Ah, well, yes, thus we have the first difficulty...'

And so went many of our lessons, each one opening up another dark crevice of ignorance which had to be lit before we could proceed further.

However, progress was made. Small steps. *Tiny* steps. But ever so slowly we ventured into areas beyond the first three letters of the alphabet. I marvelled at his patience and tenacity. He was determined not give up and went at his lessons doggedly and with stolid fortitude. The smallest hint of praise from me brought his face into a sunshine of smiles. And this was a creature close to death, or so he said, and who was I to doubt his certainty.

~~~

By the time Spring came, Rübezahl had at last managed to retain the alphabet and was even writing one or two single-syllabled words. I had had enough. I was mentally fatigued and my body was now beginning to show serious signs of wear. One chilly morning, when the sun was stealing over the landscape, I spoke for the last time to my student and my host.

'I am going now. You are well versed in the letters.'

His great brow furrowed. 'You go?'

'Yes. You must practise hard and you will soon be able to write enough words to tell those who come after how the giant Rübezahl lived on this mountain.'

Petr had arrived to take me down the mountain and I was glad to see him. I had managed to get money and a note to him about bringing some especially extra-large volumes of schoolchildren's textbooks. They were still small by Rübezahl's standards, but with care he could turn the leaves and study the words. The text was of course aimed at an infant but I told the giant, 'You have done well. If you keep up your studies you will soon be able to write your memoirs. I wish you all good will and hope the story of your life with inspire others, perhaps to live in a cave in the mountains, or to follow one of your amazing recipes for charred wild boar.' I knew I was being cruel and that he would not recognise sarcasm, but I couldn't help myself. The situation leant itself to a basin full of irony.

He thanked me, as graciously as a giant unlearned in polite manners was able to, and told me, 'You have tried hard to bore a hole in my head and pour some reading in there. It is made of rock, my brain, like my home. I thank you, my teacher. I have learned a great deal and will keep learning till I die, which will be in the first week of this year's autumn season. My life is over. I go to that place where my brothers and sisters wait for my coming. Already they are rejoicing. Goodbye then and when you read my story you will find your own name alongside mine, for it will be half yours, the tale I leave.'

I wasn't sure I wanted to be regarded as his collaborator, but he seemed to want to accord me that honour and I thanked him graciously.

Petr took me down the mountain without asking any pertinent questions and at the bottom I paid him his wages and returned to the university.

~~~

In the autumn I was told a visitor awaited me in the courtyard. I went out to find Petr standing there, cap in hand.

'He's dead,' he said, 'and he did what he wanted to do.'

I raised my eyebrows. 'He's written his life story?'

'He gave it a good try. I think you should come and look. I'll take you up there. We have to be quick as the winter will be on us soon.'

I was about to reject the offer but naturally I was curious. 'You could tell me, what he's written,' I said.

'I think you should come and see for yourself,' replied Petr.

Indeed, I felt I ought to go, out of respect for the person whose guest I had been, up in that natural fortress which had been his home.

So, two days later I once again climbed the mountain, and it took just as much of my stamina and energy as it had done the first time. I saw the cave from a distance as we approached and it looked strangely neglected. A cave is just an empty hollow in a rockface but its emptiness seemed to echo over the hillside and forests. Though the weather was mild there was a cold look to the place and the area in front of the opening appeared scruffy and unkempt.

'Where is Rübezahl's tale?' I asked. 'The story of his life.'

Petr led me to a monolith not far from the cave. I had not been expecting a great deal in the way of text since I left the giant with very limited skills. However, the brevity shocked me at first and I just stood and stared at the words, wondering why I had failed so miserably at my profession. Then gradually a change filtered through my mind until, by the time we left that inscription, I had become profoundly proud of my student. There is always to be given, with an exam that has gained very few marks for content, points for effort.

'Ten out of ten,' I murmured to Petr. 'He couldn't have tried harder. The name is especially difficult.'

There, etched deeply on the surface of the granite, were the words:

RUBEZAHL WAS HEER.
And underneath this autobiography:
R. AND F.K.

He had kept his promise and shared his achievement with his teacher.

The Goatboy and the Giant

There was a giant, full-limbed and fabulous, sleeping in the sun. The goatboy approached him warily, standing half as high as one of the enormous feet, whose bare soles looked like the bottom of a dry riverbed. When the young man walked past the towering feet he observed that the translucent moons of the creature's toenails gleamed like topaz, and the veins just beneath the surface of his delicate skin were rivers of the palest blue.

The youth began the journey from feet to head, marvelling at the paleness of the giant's body, even though it had been exposed to the fierce Turkish sun, day over day, and the abrasive sandstorms of the Turkish wilderness, night under night.

When the goatboy reached the giant's head, by way of his muscled left leg and sinewy arm, he found it to be bald. This was an old giant, one who had lost his pigtail to the passing centuries. Such ancient titans passed their final years in sleep until death came to filigree their fingers with webs, and powder their pates with fine dust.

The giant's face was turned towards the goatboy and although the creature's breath swhooshed over the wasteland, raising dust clouds and whirling widdershins, he could see it wore gentle features. The next time the giant breathed in through his nose the youth threw sand up his nostrils in order to wake him.

The giant coughed, sat up, and rubbed his face. His

eyes opened wide, then they shut tight as he gave out the most enormous sneeze, which ripped shrubs from the earth and sent them rolling like tumbleweed across the desert. Finally the giant blinked twice and looked around him.

'What time is it?' he asked, on seeing the goatboy.

'Almost the end of the century,' said the lad.

And the giant said, 'I've overslept again.'

He rose and stretched himself, then began digging, scooping out handfuls of desert sand each large enough to bury a house. The hole grew to a great pit whose sides kept flowing like a flood into its depths, but finally the giant reached water and bent his great head to suck the liquid into his mouth. When he had finished drinking the giant pulled fistfuls of cactus from the ground and chewed them to mush before swallowing. He gave one tremendous belch, wiped his mouth on his arm, then smiled at the goatboy.

'That was good,' he said, and then lay himself down once more.

'Wait!' cried the goatboy. 'You're not going back to sleep again?'

The giant sat up and blinked.

'Well, I was thinking of it, yes. I've had food and water so what else is there to stay awake for? Can you give me a shake if you come by here in a few decades?'

The goatboy folded his arms and shook his head.

His goats milled around his legs bleating as he contemplated one of the last giants left on the earth. In fact, he told himself, no one had seen such a creature for at least a hundred years. He himself was familiar with them only through the stories told him by his grandfather, back in the old township of Yozgat. He saw in this giant the potential to fulfil his ambition.

Now, the problem with goatboys was they had too much time to daydream. Once upon a century, way back before this goatboy's time, they had to fight with lion and bears, keep wolves from descending like Assyrians on the fold, defend their herd against lost armies of ravenous Greeks. When they were not looking after the goats they were practising with their slingshots or cutting new staves. Goatboys of old had no time to daydream.

Since lions, bears, wolves and confused Greeks were no longer a threat, the goatboy idled his hours away wishing he was a great rock star, like Michael Jackson, who sang to the most primitive of bushmen through the medium of transistor radios. At night the goatboy would lie under the heavens, glistening with distant suns, and think not of the wonders of the universe but of the marvellous world beyond Turkey, where a boy with something unusual to offer might become rich and famous. Goats earned him a living, but they smelled and would never lead to the kind of life a rock star followed.

'Listen,' said the goatboy to the giant, 'you and I could make a team. I bet you're the last living giant on the earth. People would pay a fortune just to look at you. We could become rich and famous together.'

'Rich and famous,' repeated the giant, using the same tremulous tones employed by the boy. 'Is that a good thing?'

'Is it a *good*? Why it's the *only* worthwhile ambition in this world. Once you're rich and famous you can do anything. I expect you could buy a bed to support your weight and drift to your final rest on a raft of duck down and goose feathers.'

The giant patted the desert sand. 'This is pretty soft,'

he murmured.

'Not as soft as a mattress stuffed with feathers,' replied the boy.

'Well, what do we have to do, to become rich and famous?' asked the giant. 'Is it hard work?'

'Certainly not. You only earn a living by working hard or providing the necessities of life, like food and water. To become rich you must peddle luxuries. You just find something people don't really need but *desire* above all else, then you sell to them at extortionate prices. I'm sure people would want to see *you* – because you're unusual in this day and age.'

'Am I?'

'Yes, and if you like I'll help you get your riches. I'll have to charge you, of course, being a professional giant manager is not an easy task. What do you say to something in the region of seventy per cent of the gross receipts?'

The giant's brow furrowed and he hugged his knees. 'What's a receipt? How many's a gross? I *don't* know anything about percentages. Are they the same as fractions?'

'I'll explain all that later,' said the goatboy, 'but in the meantime, how about it?'

'That seems fair,' the giant said. 'After all, I have no idea about how to get rich and famous, and you're an expert.'

'Precisely,' said the goatboy.

'However,' said the giant, 'I have no wish to leave this pleasant spot, even for a feather bed.' And he bid the goatboy farewell.

Stunned for only a moment, the youth invented a tale which only giants, the most gullible creatures on the earth, would believe. Unfortunately, it is a quirk of supernature, a paradox of the cruellest kind, that whatever giants believe becomes their truth.

'What was your last job?' asked the boy, knowing full well that giants never do manual work and haven't the intellect or dexterity required for other types of employment.

The giant shook his head. 'I've never had one of those.,

The goatboy opened wide his eyes in mock concern. 'You mean you've never earned anything in your life?'

'Not a penny,' confirmed the giant.

'Oh, that's really sad!'

'Now why should that be?'

'Because,' lied the boy, 'everyone knows that Og, the King of Bashan, the first giant, who walked beside Noah's Ark with his head still above water, decreed that since giants were bound to be big lazy fellows who lay around in the sun all day, those who did no work and earned nothing during their stay on earth would not be permitted to enter heaven.'

'He said that?'

'Everyone knows.'

The giant sat up and held his face in his great hands, looking down through his fingers at the tiny goatboy below. His eyes were like lakes with no finite depth. His brow was a furrowed field. His pink lips trembled with worry. 'I haven't earned a penny,' he cried, 'so I shall never get to heaven.'

In believing the tale it had become the truth.

'You still have time before you die,' said the goatboy, 'to redeem yourself. Follow me!'

So the giant got to his feet and carried the goatboy down to the coast, striding out across the wasteland, each stride being twenty-one miles in length. Once they reached the sea, the goatboy instructed the giant to go into the water and follow the shoreline round to Istanbul, where he hoped they would be able to start making their fortune. It was not possible for the giant to walk over the land because there were cities, towns, villages and farms scattered all over the countryside and there was a danger someone might be crushed beneath those great soles. Even so, they had to keep a sharp lookout for ships, cruising along in the shallows, and fisherfolk collecting their lobsterpots out on the mud.

When they reached Istanbul, the giant was amazed at the amount of building that had gone on while he had been away. 'This was only a village last time I was here,' he said. I can't even recognise it. Are you sure this is Byzantium?'

'It was called that,' said the boy, 'but they changed the name to Constantinople and now it's Istanbul.'

'I'd never have believed it,' said the giant.

'What can I say?' replied the goatboy. 'You've been a bit of a sluggard in the past.'

'I suppose that's true, but I do like my sleep.'

'Well, that's going to change for a while, but eventually it will be worth it. You'll have your feather bed to float to heaven on and I can start my career as a rock star with a solid financial backing. What we'll do is sound out the city's businessmen. You'll have to wait here while I go and make some arrangements.'

'All right,' said the giant, who was up to his waist in harbour water, the ships circumnavigating his girth. He folded his arms, to keep his hands from doing any damage, and set himself four-square in the mud. It began to rain, something the giant had not experienced while out in the desert, but he did not complain. He knew the goatboy was helping him to a better way of rest.

It drizzled for days on end and the winds came from the north, but the giant merely shivered and hugged his beautiful body with his arms, trusting that the boy would soon return and help him earn some money so that Og would let him into heaven.

The goatboy left his fabulous creature and went to the big corporations, saying he had something quite extraordinary to offer them in the way of show business. Eventually he found himself in a plush office confronted by an array of the most-wealthy persons in Istanbul. He explained his proposition to them.

'What I have here is probably unique,' he said. 'A giant, ladies and gentleman, in an age when technology is becoming old hat. People are beginning to get bored with video games and computers and are starting to look to the past, the golden age, the antique era, the ancient civilizations. What we have here is a wonder of the old world, when fables and folk tales were live entertainment.'

He paused to see how his speech was affecting his audience. They did not appear spellbound. In fact, someone yawned.

'Just what,' rumbled one bearded moneyman, 'do you propose to *do* with your giant?'

'Why,' cried the goatboy, 'people will pay just to look at him.'

The old gentleman nodded towards the window overlooking the harbour.

'Why should they? They can see him for free. You can't miss him, can you? He's the tallest thing for miles.'

'We'll have to hide him in a building so that they

can't see him for free,' said the boy frantically, feeling that things were not working out as well as he had planned, and his millions were slipping away from him. 'I mean, if they can't see him they'll pay then, won't they?'

'It'll take years to build something to contain your giant,' snapped one of the other financiers in the room, 'and where would we put him in the meantime? There'll be tourists descending on Istanbul like locusts before we get him hidden from sight, which will be good for the city but not for the owners of the giant. The Japanese and Americans and Germans will all have seen him by the time we get him under cover. The British think they've got the most interesting weather in the world, and don't bother with any other wonder of nature. The Scandinavians and Russians are too phlegmatic to concern themselves with fabulous creatures. The French don't like anything they haven't discovered themselves. The Koreans would pirate holograms of him all over the world. The Swiss prefer clockwork giants about six inches high that they can sell to the toyshops. The Chinese haven't got any money and the Africans don't like to travel. The rest of Asia is too busy trying to catch up with the century. That leaves the Australians and New Zealanders, who don't amount to more than a handful of backpackers who prefer cheap boarding houses and food from the stalls in the all-night markets. Need I go on? Good morning to you, young man.'

And so, to his dismay, the goatboy was dismissed.

Instead of returning to the giant and reporting his failure to the creature, he went on a tour of all the major cities in Turkey, trying to drum up enough enthusiasm to take the giant on a roadshow. He wrote to the

Rolling Stones, telling them the giant would make a wonderful backdrop to their next concert. He tried to call David Bowie, who might have been able to suggest some zany use for the muscled colossus. He visited local radio and TV stations and went on the air with news of his find. All ended in failure.

'Can he sing?' asked the agents. 'What does he play?'

Finally, defeat bearing down on him with its distinctively heavy and lumpy form, the goatboy returned to the Istanbul harbour.

There he found that his living wonder had caught a cold from standing in the wet, in the wind, and in the rain, which had turned to pneumonia. The poor giant had expired, slipping down into the waters of the Bosporus and floating away on the tide, out into the sea of Marmara where he drifted finally into the Mediterranean itself. His beautiful big body was washed up on the shores of a land whose inhabitants had stopped believing in giants and they were both amazed and confounded by his presence on their beach. For a while the people took to travelling down to the coast to view his remains and have their photographs taken, standing between his fingers. A famous writer came to write descriptive notes on how the drowned giant affected the local population.

In time, his great ribs were used as bridges to cross ornamental streams, his pelvis became a skateboard park for the young and agile, his spinal column became a tunnel down which youngsters would slide, his legbones and arm bones were trestles for swings, his hands and feet seats for the elderly.

There was a small charge for the use of these facilities.

The Grootslang

Not all giants are tall. Some are long. Not all giants stand vertically. Some make their way horizontally. The Grootslang was a long horizontal giant.

~~~

The place was South Africa, and the time was just after the Anglo-Zulu Wars and not long before the war with the Boers in the same region. The man was a Welsh infantryman who went by the name of 637 Jones. That's more than a name, but he'd been a soldier for so long he'd grown used to the prefix. He'd fought under it, been wounded under it. Way back in time he'd been promoted to the rank of corporal but was demoted for insolence and insubordination, so went swiftly back to Private 637 Jones.

Like many warriors, those he fought and killed he did not hate. Those he went into battle for, he didn't love. He particularly admired the Zulus even though they'd slaughtered his comrades at Isandlwana. Two thousand soldiers had fallen that day, including several ten-year-old drummer boys. The men and youths of King Cetshwayo's impi had died too: twenty thousand brave warriors threw themselves into the hail of fire from Martini-Henry rifles. And they died in as many thousands, having only hide shields as a defence against the hail of lead that ripped into them. The Zulus had triumphed and 637 was one of only a clutch of soldiers who'd managed to survive the black onslaught.

Unlike the British government and public, 637 did not regard it as a British defeat. It was to him a Zulu victory. Lord Chelmsford, the commander who'd made the mistake of splitting his army into two, later made sure that King Cetshwayo and his Zulu nation were severely punished for their audacity. Despite that, there was no escaping the Englishman's place in history, for King Cetshwayo had bestowed upon Chelmsford the unwelcome honour of commanding the worst trouncing received by the British army in a war against men armed only with spears and clubs. Lord Chelmsford was unsurprisingly somewhat bitter about the fact. However, 637 Jones felt no pity for him. He regarded his leader as a war-loving ambitious, ruthless toff.

637's service time in the army came to a halt while the 24th Foot was still in South Africa awaiting repatriation. He could have returned with his regiment but decided to stay in South Africa. He'd heard of a giant snake – the Grootslang in Afrikaans – which was as long as a Cardiff street. In the middle, its girth rivalled that of a pregnant elephant's. The Grootslang could travel at enormous speeds over flat ground and was able to rear like a king cobra and peer down upon its prey from the height of a baobab tree.

637 Jones was no zoologist or lover of serpents in general, unlike an aristocratic subaltern in his regiment who collected everything from beetles to buffalos. No, one of the reasons he'd joined the army was to get away from herding sheep on the Welsh rain-sodden hills. He'd heard that this giant snake, whose jaws could open wide enough to swallow a standing man complete with hat and boots, was a collector of gems. Its cave, called the Wonder Hole, was said to be full of

diamonds, emeralds, sapphires and opals – any bright and lustrous jewel. It was known to be able not only to see such jewels from a vast distance, but also to *smell* them. The Grootslang also had one great talent unique among snakes: it could sing. Oh, not in any known language, or even with the sweet trilling of birds, but with deep hollow tones that could drown the howling of wolves.

Now dressed in the floppy wide-brimmed hat of the Boer farmers, and plain grey trousers and shirt, 637 no longer looked like a veteran soldier. His skin, which had reddened under the African sun on arrival on that continent, was now a deep mahogany brown. He was a smallish man, with dark hair and blue eyes, but stocky and formidable in a fight when his fists became flails. An average shot with a rifle, he'd somehow managed to retain his army 450 Martini-Henry and a good supply of ammunition. If he were to cross the country, east to west, to Richtersveld, home of the Nama people, he might come across Zulus who held a grudge. He'd be a white man alone except for his native companion.

Mati was an amaNgwane tribesman who had fought for the British in the Natal Native Contingent. The amaNgwane were traditional enemies of the Zulus and 637 Jones and his friend Mati would suffer the same fate should they meet with any grudge holders, despite the differences in their skin and culture.

The pair set off one morning on foot from Durban, leading a pack mule carrying their supplies.

'It's hot,' grumbled 637.

'You say that always,' replied Mati, 'but it is not. It is winter. You say hot but wait when we get to where we go. Come the summer, you fry like an ostrich egg.'

'How long will it take to get there?'

Mati shrugged. 'How fast will we go? If it is only me, fourteen, maybe fifteen days – but you? Small legs?'

'Listen boyo, I've just spent eighteen years with the British army, marching at the double across wide continents. I can do what you can do and some more.'

'Yes, but can you cook?'

637 was mystified. 'What's that got to do with anything?'

'You have to eat, or you die.'

This was turning into one of those discussions he used to have with his wife when she was alive. The subject would subtly change as the argument went along and he found himself ever on the defensive. He decided to hold his tongue before he became frustrated and began shouting. Mati did not like anyone shouting at him, any more than 637's wife had done. Bethan would lapse into a smouldering silence for at least a day. Mati, on the other hand, would start shouting back in his own language which sounded much more threatening than either Welsh or English, the only two languages 637 had at his command.

The journey would not be overly long, as journeys in foreign lands went, but it would be difficult. There were rivers to cross, mountain ranges to navigate, deserts and harsh terrains to trek. Their path would take them through five different lands or states: Natal, Basutoland, the Orange Free State, Bechuanaland and finally into Richtersfeld. Richtersfeld itself was mainly mountainous desert, desolate and forbidding. It was, however, the home of the Grootslang and so the most necessary landscape to traverse.

Even before they had left Natal the Welshman encountered a snake. It was coiled around a cold cooking pot when he woke on the second morning. 637 Jones had seen several snakes, including the deadly Cape Cobra, while serving with the army in Africa and India, but on being surprised by one – he was almost always surprised – he felt a chill run through his body. He gasped loudly enough to wake Mati who, when he saw the creature, laughed.

'Karoo snake,' he said. 'Nothing to harm you.'

'Harmless? Are you sure?'

'Listen boss, this tiny snake makes like the little finger of the Grootslang – how will you be when you see the Grootslang?'

'Snakes don't have fingers,' muttered 637.

Mati shook his head and went to make breakfast, shooing the offending reptile off his kitchen utensil. 637 watched the thing slide away over the dust, thinking that at a yard long it wasn't *so* damn tiny.

When they entered Basutoland the going was fairly gentle, though there were several fast rivers to cross. They headed for the Maloti Mountains, a spur of the Drakensberg range, but over undulating grasslands which distracted the pack mule who kept coming stubbornly to a halt in order to graze. There were scattered trees, mostly willow of some kind. Mati collected cheche bush for fuel for the fire. Hunting was easy too, with antelope and hares. 637 Jones asked Mati why the 'deer' didn't seem to be wary of lions, but the amaNgwane told him the last lion in that area had been killed. 637 didn't enquire whether that was because of white hunters or perhaps an initiation ceremony for local youths. He believed it was probably the former. They saw zebra everywhere and wildebeest, which like the antelope didn't seem concerned about predators. 637 wondered about leopards on the grasslands.

The ex-soldier got a shock when they came to the mountains and they started to climb up to the passes. It was very cold, with snow and ice shrouding the rock. A single night up in heights froze him to the core. He was never so glad as when they descended to the Orange Free State. Even this was on a plateau some six-hundred feet above sea level. There were farms scattered on the bush veld. The Orange River ran through the landscape, a place where wild dogs seem to be everywhere. Here 637 met with his first big beast encounter.

He'd gone down to the river to get water, while Mati lit a fire. Having dipped the two containers in river and filled them he stood up and turned to find himself not far from a rhino that had come down to water itself. 637 froze. He knew rhinos were poorly sighted, but did they have a good sense of smell? 637 was inclined to think they probably did, since in nature poor eyesight was almost always compensated with another of the senses.

He stood, still as a stone, staring at the beast which was only twenty yards away to his right. The rhino lifted its head, once or twice, and swayed it from side to side. 637 held his breath during these movements and kept praying silently to himself, *Please God, don't let him turn this way when he leaves*. 637 was not a great lover of chapel but we tend to turn to the Almighty in times of great peril, even if we don't believe in him. Finally, the great white beast turned right round, stared into the middle distance for a few moments, then lumbered off towards some thorn trees. 637 let out a gasp and his shoulders slumped.

He looked up at the sky and nodded.

Just as he was turning to go back to the night camp, something caught his eye. There, in the shadows of an acacia stood a man with a rifle in the crook of his arm. He was staring hard at 637 Jones who, once his surprise was under control, stared back with equal ferocity. The man walked slowly towards him. He looked tall and willowy, his clothes hanging loosely from him, the broad-brimmed Boer farmer's hat shielding large ears and a long narrow nose.

'Who the hell are you?'

The words were in clipped accents.

'Jones,' answered 637, 'late of Her Majesty's army. You're a *yarpie*?'

The man's head jerked back and he dropped his rifle into his right hand.

'We don't like that expression, *rooinek*.'

'What's wrong with *yarpie*? I thought it meant an Afrikaner farmer.'

'It's offensive.'

'So's red-neck. My neck's as brown as yours, boyo.'

The farmer stared at him for a while, then said, 'What are you doing here, man? This is my land.'

'I've been fighting bloody Zulus.'

The farmer smirked. 'I heard. Gave you a lickin', eh?'

637 knew that the Boers had successfully defended themselves in a battle against fifteen thousand Zulus at the Battle of Blood River, and with old-fashioned muzzle-loaders, not modern Martini-Henrys.

'Yes, they did. Good fighters, the Zulus.'

The farmer shrugged. 'I still haven't heard what you're doing wandering all over my land.'

'Passing through. Just passing through. On my way to chapel.'

The Boer looked mystified. 'I don't know what that means, but you better go on your way bloody quick. You were lucky with that rhino, man.'

'You would have shot him.'

'Not with this,' replied the Boer, gesturing with his weapon. 'I can hit a fly on a tree branch with it, but it won't stop a big bastard like that one. On your way then, *rooinek*. If you get stopped by anyone else you better tell them Janco Van der Plume let you through. Keep going. We're not fond of you English.'

'And that's another thing, boyo,' replied 637, walking away, 'I'm not bloody English.'

Mati laughed when 637 told him of his encounter with the farmer.

'They do not like you, much, the Boers.'

'So he said,' replied 637, 'last thing.'

~~~

The pair struck camp and were on their way 'bloody quick' in the long shadow of the Drakensbergs, which rose west to east. Most of the journey on the Highveld Plateau was through bush country with eland and black wildebeest scattered over its landscape. They entered Bechuanaland, having to cross the southern tip of that country. This was British-ruled territory, and the Tswana people were friendly. Mati and 637 stocked up on their supplies before finally walking into the arid wilderness of Richtersveld, home of the Grootslang.

637 stared at the desolate and forbidding mountainous desert region that spread out on all sides. 'Well, here's a patch of hell for you,' he muttered. 'Desert I heard it might be, but there's more dunes on

the Gower than in this place. Who did you say lived here, Mati?'

'Nama people.'

'Oh yes. Nomads. Animal skin tents thrown over poles. Bloody good luck to them, I say. We'll do what we came to do, make ourselves wealthy, then get out, as quick as you like. Tomorrow we'll talk to someone about finding the Wonder Hole – there's posh for you, that name, eh? Probably some stinking cave in this yellow and red dust that's been choking our pack mule for the last few miles. What a place live! Bottom of the barrel when it comes to it. Nothing but stark rock and … what the fuck is that?' he cried, stepping back and pointing at a thorny-looking creature peering at him from a rock.

'Spiny lizard,' replied Mati. 'Ugly, eh?'

'Scary.'

'Scared of a lizard? What happens when you see the big snake?'

'I'll be terrified, but hopefully near to becoming rich.'

~~~

The next day they went in search of the Nama. 637 could not believe how bleak and hostile the landscape was. It filled his spirit with depression and dread. How could anyone live in such a place? However, they did, somehow, and Mati found them. The amaNgwane prised the location of the Grootslang's cave out of some unwilling mouths.

The fortune hunters then set out to camp on a peak two miles away from the cave of the beast where 637 could watch through his binocular telescope. They were there several days before they saw the giant snake emerge from its lair and the hairs on the back of the Welshman's neck rose in response.

'Shit!' he said, staring through the glasses. 'It's huge.'

Mati raised his eyebrows as if to say, what did you expect?

The Grootslang was indeed a monster. They heard it before seeing it. Its operatic songs filled the evening hills. As long as a railway train and just as fat. It was a filthy dark yellow in colour with black markings like magic symbols all along its scaly back. The eyes were also yellow, bright and terrifying to look at. Then there was that forked tongue, which lashed like a six-foot-long whip from its foul mouth. When it opened its huge jaws the fangs caught the sunlight and flashed like swords. This diamond-loving serpent, this blunder of the gods, needed no venom to disable its prey. It could crush a boulder with those coils and swallow a hippo with one bite. A fearsome creature that filled both Mati and 637 with a strong desire to return to a place of safety.

'We'll see how long it stays out of its cave,' said 637, 'then when it goes out again, we'll sneak into that treasure trove and steal what we can carry.'

'Not me,' said Mati, firmly. 'You go alone.'

'What?' cried the ex-soldier. 'You don't want any gems?'

'Only payment for services, not for to be swallowed.'

'Huh! You're a coward.'

'That word only works on a white man,' replied his partner complacently. 'It mean nothing to ama-Ngwane. When we run away, we praise each other for being wise.'

'The NNC didn't run at Isandlwana. They were

massacred by the Zulus, just like the white soldiers. I know you weren't there. You went with Chelmsford when he split the army, but just the same...'

'My cousin was at Isandlwana. He did not run. I know why he did not run.'

'Why?'

'He could not escape. If he run away the Zulus run after him and catch him and kill him anyway. How many of you escape? Not many. You think we are stupid because we are not like you? We have a brain like all men, white, black or brown. We do not always think in the same way, that's all.'

'I don't think you're stupid,' replied 637, loading the pack mule. 'There *are* some of my people who do, but *they're* the stupid ones.'

~~~

So, when the time came, 637 went to the cave alone, leading the pack mule. He carried an oil lamp, his rifle, and two bottles which were in holsters on his belt. He'd left Mati with the field glasses so that his companion could signal to him if the Grootslang returned while he was in its lair. He was trembling with fear even though he had watched the Grootslang slither out of sight between two mountains.

He left the mule at the entrance to the cave and began his search for the fabulous treasure of the giant snake. There was a dim light in a large cavern, coming from the cave's entrance, but he needed the lamp for the dark corners and crevices.

Some of his fellow soldiers back in the regiment were convinced this story about a giant snake and its treasure was all a myth. Others, locals, had sworn it was true. 637 had been inclined to believe those who lived in the country rather than those who were there for a brief visit. And the monster was here, so why not a vast fortune in precious stones? There were male birds which collected pretty trinkets to assist them in mating with a female. Magpies, for instance, adorned their nests with shiny objects.

A giant snake in a God-awful miserable-looking land might also want to brighten its lair to lift its slimy spirits.

Everything he'd been told about this fortune had fired him with a desire to grab as much of it as he could carry, or rather his mule could carry, yet to try not to be too greedy. Two saddlebags full would be enough, more than enough, to make him wealthy for the rest of his life. He knew he mustn't let the sight of so many glittering precious stones turn his head. Gold fever, diamond fever, could be the death of a man. Keep calm and cool, and fight down the craze to own all that was there. That was his resolve.

Except there was *nothing* here.

Not a bright stone of any kind. Just rock and dust, and old bones. Bits of animal skin too, cluttering the darkness, which on inspection also contained human clothing. Rags and bones. Nothing of any real value or worth.

He yelled his frustration until it echoed throughout the cavern and the sound hurt his ears and destroyed those wild expectations he had nursed for so long. If he had not given way to anger and anguish he would have heard the warning whistle from Mati, telling him the snake was returning. It was only when the mule bolted that he realised something was wrong. But before he himself could run from the cave the daylight at the entrance turned to darkness. He was trapped and so scrambled to the furthest reaches of a large cavern where he found a fissure in the rock wall. Throwing the oil lamp away, he squeezed inside a gap just big enough to house a small stocky man. There he stayed, praying the Grootslang would not find his hiding place.

It was a forlorn hope. It knew something was in its lair. It opened its mouth and sang in a low-mellow tones. Its thick coils seem to fill the whole cavern as it writhed and twisted, its horrible massive blunt snout sniffing the rocky interior of its home. The plaintive notes filled the caverns and it seemed to 637 that the echoes bounced around the rock walls for a long time. Then the Grootslang began to search every corner until finally it found him. There the monster ceased crooning and worked at trying to winkle 637 Jones out and swallow him whole. It worked at it for an hour until the great snake retreated a few yards, but remained with its eyes on its prey, the ex-choirboy, ex-coalminer, ex-soldier, ex-snake-hunter, 637 Jones.

There it stayed with great patience, occasionally lashing the crevice with its tongue. This went on for a long time, until suddenly the snake began to gag violently as if it were choking. 637 watched in hope. Was the creature ill? It was said to be very old. Hundreds of years old. Nothing lived forever, did it? Not even mistakes left in the wilderness by the gods.

But then the monster let out a huge cough, vomiting a pile of bones. 637 stared in horror at the heap on the floor.

There were two human skulls among them, one of normal adult size, the other much smaller.

'If that big one belongs to my friend,' snarled 637, 'I swear I'll come back from the dead and hack that ugly head off.'

It was a stupid remark, but it put fire into his blood.

637 had dropped his rifle in the scramble to find a hiding place. Otherwise, he'd have shot the beast in the eye. Now he started thinking more clearly. He carefully removed one of the bottles from its holster. The vessel was full of black powder and nails. It also had a piece of towelling for a fuse. He reached awkwardly into a breast pocket and withdrew a box of matches. Fumbling in the tight space, he lit the fuse. The full glare of those yellow serpentine eyes were focussed on the flame, fascinated by it, and then seemingly disappointed when it went out. While the fuse slowly burned its way down to the bottle's neck 637 opened his mouth and began to sing 'Men of Harlech' in that wonderful baritone for which many Welshmen are famed.

The Grootslang was like a parlour dog, unable to resist joining him in singing a duet. It opened cavernous jaws, lined with stalactites and stalagmites, and let out a beautiful but unholy howling, managing to follow the Welshman's tune. Its pitch was perfect and it was soon in unison with the human singer, although in a different but complimentary octave.

637 almost felt sorry for what he was about to do to his musical companion, but then remembered the human bones scattered about the cavern. The Welshman's heart was beating wildly as he tossed the homemade grenade deep into the throat of the monster. The Grootslang swallowed involuntarily. A moment later there was a muffled explosion. The Grootslang's neck bulged and the creature let out a deafening unmelodic cry of despair.

It squirmed and rolled for a while on the dusty cave floor before the light in its eyes dimmed and it lay still.

~~~

Once the pair had returned to Durban, 637 promised Mati he would send him money when he got back to Britain. Mati shook hands with the ex-soldier and they parted on the quay. When he reached London, 637, now plain Dyfed Jones, went to the British Museum followed by an enormous travelling trunk. There he sold a massive snakeskin to the museum. The sum was very large, due to the uniqueness of the reptile who'd worn it in life. Mati was not forgotten of course, and his share transferred to him. The bonus for 637 was that the museum authorities and London's Royal Society were also keen to have this small dark-haired man as a paid speaker at their establishments in the future. America remained a promise, as did Paris, Milan and Berlin. With a single exploit, Dyfed Jones had managed to jump up the social ladder almost to the top.

One big snake for the museum, one giant leap for 637.

Brobdingnag II

The species, known throughout the Canis Major galaxy as humans, are a curious but lethal vermin. They get everywhere, get into everything, and always end up destroying any planet on which their swarms choose to settle. Destroying, in the sense they leave it barren and lifeless, abandoning it, and then going on to find other worlds to infest and repeat the crime.

MacEscobar and his crew were scouts searching for such worlds. It was a dangerous job because the reputation of human beings had spread rapidly throughout Canis Major. The humans had long ago left behind them the Milky Way, absolutely devoid of even the barest chance of vascular plants reviving any previously hospitable planet therein. Those worlds bearing intelligent life in the Canis Major galaxy have since swiftly armed themselves.

There were three other members of the crew, besides MacEscobar: O'Gotti, Parkerson and Ben Dillinger. As individuals, they had a variety of duties on board the ship and another set when they landed on a planet that looked like it was worth stealing and exploiting. They wouldn't be the ones to do the dirty deed, of course, and there would be many, many promises that this time, this time, they and their descendants would not get greedy and would treat this precious chunk of rock with care and respect. They would not strip mine it of all its minerals. They would not poison its atmosphere with noxious gases. They would not slash and burn their way over its surface. They would not kill all of its other lifeforms. They would not leave it a charred lump of clinker and fuck the hell off without a backward glance to find another jewel to tarnish.

Promises. Promises.

'What do you reckon,' said MacEscobar, staring at the lush growth of the rain forest. 'Promising?'

Parkerson, female of the species, sniffed the atmosphere. 'Oxygen. Quite heady, actually. Water – you saw that sea when we descended. Plenty of plant life and I wouldn't be surprised if there's plenty of animal life too. This could be it. It's what we've been looking for.'

O'Gotti nodded his approval.

'We could make this ours,' said Ben Dillinger. 'Let's do a cursory explore and then if it comes up to its promise, hand it over to the terraformers.'

Now, ever since the first bunch of humans decided to move home and occupy a territory in which none of them were born, they have chosen one of two well-tried methods to make it their own: *commerce* or *conquest.* They either began by trading with whomever had been born on that particular patch of ground, then sneaked themselves in gradually until they took the place over, or – the shorter, quicker method of stealing land – they went in with weapons blazing and wiped out or subdued the current owners.

Here are two good examples of these methods.

There was once a group of humans called the Portuguese. They were particularly good at the former method, devised by one of their number, Henry the Navigator. They traded with the indigenous population, then after a while applied to have warehouses on the shore of that terrain. Thereafter they built more structures, imported more staff, until they were thoroughly embedded.

The Spanish, however, went in led by a warrior called Cortes, with horses, guns and swords, and simply killed and killed until they were the masters and had enslaved all the remaining indigenists.

This is not say those two groups were the only peoples to use such methods. Other groups had done so before them and even more did so afterwards. In those times, way back in history, humans were colonising each other's patches of land on a single world. Later, of course, those patches became whole planets, which is where we are today. When it was just an area on the same world, the indigenous population, or what was left of them, could become absorbed into the newcomer's society. When that new piece of land became a planet there was little or no possibility of two quite different life-forms copulating. The humans either wiped out the local population or herded them into barely habitable corners of their legitimate birthplace. That planet would then be denuded before the humans moved on to another.

~~~

Leaving behind O'Gotti to guard the ship, MacEscobar, Parkerson and Ben Dillinger set out, armed to the teeth, to investigate this new world. MacEscobar was eager to make a good showing with this mission. They were threatening him with a desk job, and he believed himself too big for that. He was a scout and scouts are out in the field. They are the gung-ho bastards with guts and heart, which every schoolchild admires and wants to emulate. Adventurers. Wilders, shooting off into the unknown to grab worlds for the human race. They didn't come any tougher or any harder than the scouts. Desk jobs were for pussies, for old men and women whose bladders had gone to pot. MacEscobar was going to prove, with this mission, that he could still cut it for the benefit of the lard-arses who wanted to stay in one place and live boring uneventful lives.

~~~

The trees and plants, the crew noticed, were massively tall and thick, but they found wide tracks to follow through them. The tracks looked as if they had been made by a creature with tools. Parkerson had a device for detecting animal life and the dial was whizzing round like mad. She had no need to tell the other two that there were sentient beings close by. The three humans slowed their pace and looked around them, studying the undergrowth and the canopy of the forest. Insects the size of a human foot were scuttling back and forth. A massive bird-like creature flew overhead, blocking out the light from one of the twin suns.

'What do you think,' asked Ben Dillinger, 'should we continue?'

Before either of his companions had time to answer, the tall blades of foliage on the right side of the track parted. A furry snout appeared, higher than a human head. Then the rest of the face, with two dark round eyes. MacEscobar and his crew froze. They already had weapons in their hands, but they kept perfectly still as the creature emerged. It stopped halfway out of the trees, sniffed loudly, and turned its head towards the humans. They held their breath and Ben Dillinger slowly raised his weapon. However, after a few moments the creature turned its gaze away, then shuffled on short legs across the track and disappeared into the undergrowth on the other side.

'Shit!' whispered Parkerson. 'That was a big one.'

'Did you record that?' asked Ben Dillinger of his captain.

MacEscobar nodded. 'Yes, I did.'

'Okay, before we go any further, let's find out what it might be so we can know whether it's carnivorous or a herbivore. What's the analysis?'

Parkerson: 'I would like to know that.'

MacEscobar fiddled with the controls on his weapon. He studied the image that appeared on its screen. Then he shook his head as if in disbelief.

'Well?' asked Ben Dillinger.

'The nearest the Diagnoster can get to it is an animal they had on the planet Earth, way back when.'

'Which is?' asked Parkerson.

'It was called a "hedgehog", a sort of spiny mammal. The hedgehog was an omnivore and there's no reason not to suspect this one is too.'

'So, it could devour us, if it chose to?'

'It would seem so,' replied MacEscobar, 'but that's not what worries me overmuch. I mean, we could probably kill it very easily. It's made of flesh and bone. But was does concern me…' He paused long enough for Ben Dillinger to interject.

'I know what you're getting at. It's covered in spines. Those spines are armour. It needs them to protect itself against a larger, more ferocious creature, and evolution has given it those spines to ward off predators. That hedgehog is no doubt prey to more than one hunter. I say we go back to the ship now and blast off. Let's have a good look around from the safety of the air.'

MacEscobar agreed with a nod of his head. They hurried back along the track but when they reached the clearing where they had parked the ship, there was nothing to see but burnt foliage. All three stared in disbelief. MacEscobar reached for his comm and tried to raise O'Gotti. There was no answer. Not a click or a ding to indicate that a connection had been made. Not even a crackle or a hiss of white noise. Nothing but silence.

Parkerson: 'O'Gotti would answer if he was able to.'

'Of course he would,' cried Ben Dillinger. 'And why would he take off without us?'

MacEscobar: 'Unless he panicked. Maybe he was attacked by something he knew he couldn't handle.'

'Or,' came back Ben Dillinger, 'the something that attacked him was able to pick up the ship and carry it off?'

The three of them stood immobile, then MacEscobar shivered. They were all thinking, *Was there some creature THAT large on the planet?*

MacEscobar again: 'Let's not rush to any conclusions. Look around, see if there are any prints on the ground. Any clues.' He looked round at the rainforest behind them. 'We didn't hear anything come crashing through the trees. Maybe he did take off for some reason and intends returning soon to pick us up. Maybe the comm isn't working at all. We've had that happen before, haven't we?'

'No,' muttered Parkerson and no one argued with her.

Ben Dillinger: 'I say we wait here. Keep our eyes wide open for any wildlife and sit tight until O'Gotti decides to return.'

They found some rocks to sit tight on and wait.

After quite a while the giant hedgehog reappeared, but once again it didn't seem to be at all interested in the humans. It had a huge worm in its jaws which was wrestling with the hedgehog's nose. The size of the worm did nothing to calm the feelings of the crew. Ben Dillinger said in a quiet strained voice, 'We might end up having to eat one of those too.'

MacEscobar spent the next hour or two before evening arrived retrying the comm, but without success.

~~~

Night came without any further visiting giants. However, it did bring sounds. Loud ones with jungle tones. Giant monkeys? Giant big cats? Giant constrictor snakes? Imaginations ran riot.

Dawn brought no ship and therefore no relief. Ben Dillinger checked his boots for scorpions and then realised he was wasting his time. Any scorpion would be bigger than his boot. He was hungry and thirsty now and suggested someone should go out and look for food.

MacEscobar: 'Good idea.'

'Let's face it,' moaned Ben Dillinger, 'if O'Gotti is not back by now, he's not coming.'

MacEscobar: 'We don't know that. Parkerson, let's you and I go and see if we can find something that looks edible, and maybe some water. Ben Dillinger, you stay here in case O'Gotti does come back. While we're gone, get on the comm and see if you can raise anyone, anyone at all. There may be another ship nearby.'

So far, MacEscobar had avoided sending out a general interplanetary mayday signal. There was no indication that any of the crew had met with serious harm and there was one's personal credibility to protect. MacEscobar did not want to be made the laughingstock of the scout fleet by calling for immediate assistance when such a thing might later be proved to be totally unnecessary. So far, they had seen a giant mammal which appeared to be benign towards humans. Oh, and a rather large worm. Yes, naturally that sighting would form the backbone of any gossip being exchanged among rival crews.

How many scoleciphobics does it take to send out a mayday signal? Just one and his name is MacEscobar. Oh, ha ha. That would be funny.

The two set out and scoured the nearby rainforest, finding very little that looked edible. There was a fruit which looked something like an apple. The Analyser informed them it was safe to eat. When Parkerson bit into it though, it disintegrated into powder, like a fungoid puffball. They did manage to find a clearwater stream which on testing proved it to be drinkable. The energy fluid in their flasks had been drunk so they filled the flasks with the water.

On the way back to the place where Ben Dillinger was waiting they heard him scream. Running to the fringe of the forest they could see their crewmate was crawling with monstrous black insects with pincers the size of pinking shears. Even before they got halfway to him, the screaming had ceased and his body crumpled to the ground. Within a few more seconds his skeleton was visible to his comrades, who promptly turned and ran back into the rainforest. Now MacEscobar couldn't get the comm out of his backpack fast enough.

'Mayday, mayday, mayday,' he called. 'Is there anyone near coordinates…' And he pressed the button which automatically sent out the position of the planet in the solar system, followed by the position of that system in the galaxy and finally the position of the caller on the planet. Any scout ships, or indeed a station on a planet or moon within reach, would answer the call for help. All MacEscobar and Parkerson had to do was stay alive until they arrived. O'Gotti too, if he was still breathing the rich oxygenated air of the planet Parkerson had, in her lighter moment, christened *Brobdingnag*.

MacEscobar and Parkerson found it difficult to just stand still on the edge of the rainforest and listen for the rescue craft. They didn't want to go all the way out into the open because they would be visible to any hungry creature which was happy to work for its supper. Humans on a quest for another world to destroy are usually wrapped in several layers of fibrous material reinforced with bits of metal. A carnivore like a wolf or big cat might be put off after the first couple of bites, whereas a crocodile would possibly spend a bit of time opening the parcel to see what was inside. The ant-like creatures that had eaten Ben Dillinger had somehow managed to get through the packaging, probably by first thinking that the stuff they were chewing would make a good lining for their nest and then when they reached the meat were happily surprised.

So, the pair wandered around the forest, pale eyes wide open for any danger. It wasn't long before they came across some huge but shapeless prints in the dust. It was difficult to make out what owned that spoor because the surface in that area, under the dust, was rock. All that could be ascertained was that the thin layer of dust had been displaced at regular intervals.

MacEscobar told Parkerson to wait and watch for the rescue, while he warily followed the marks until they went into the trees. He was still curious about the type of any creature larger than the hedgehog they'd seen. However, he saw nothing really alarming. No monstrous big cats or ravenous canines. He didn't doubt there were some on the planet, so he remained on his guard.

As he returned to Parkerson by a slightly different route, he was suddenly aware the substance of the ground beneath feet had changed. Looking down, he realised he was walking on metal. It shone like a silver pond. MacEscobar swallowed hard as he recognised what it was – the ship that had carried him to this god-awful planet – flattened into a single bright silver sheet. There was the distinct possibility, a *probability*, that the body of O'Gotti was inside that metal pancake, having been squashed between the walls of the ship.

'Fuck!' MacEscobar whispered.

He whispered in case there was the something nearby capable of treading on a spaceship and turning it into a flattened drink can. This world was a nightmare. Could they, with the right number of immigrants bearing the latest weapons that ingenuity had to offer – always a plus when it came to humans – could they turn this planet into a liveable and pleasant world on which to live? He doubted it. There would have to be a mass slaughter of insects for a start, wouldn't there? As MacEscobar made his way back to Parkerson, he checked what was the likely number of insects on an Earth-like world. The device told him that at any one time in its history Earth had had in the region of 10,000,000,000,000,000,000 individual insects living in the cracks and chinks of the landscape.

'What? What? Forget it pal,' he murmured, putting the device back in his pack. 'Fuck this for a game of soldiers. I'm going to take that desk job. Get me out of here. Get me the fuck off this bastard planet. I've had enough. I'm done. I've given it my best and I'm...' He stopped dead in his sentence and in his tracks – and stared at the sight which turned his stomach.

'Oh, God, no. Not you too, Parkerson?'

Out in a patch of open ground was the giant hedgehog. It was lying on its side with a blistered face. It would appear it had attacked Parkerson, who would not have blasted it otherwise. She was not the sort of scout who would kill for the pleasure or for anything but food or to protect herself. Indeed, she had allowed the spiny beast to get too close to her. It had rolled over her in its death throes and she had been impaled. The spines had pierced right through her body and the points were dripping with her blood. It must have been a quick death because he hadn't been gone long.

The hedgehog's protective weapons had left her a gherkin full of cocktail sticks.

~~~

MacEscobar was rescued a short while later. He did indeed get his desk job. As previously indicated, MacEscobar's comrades were a rough, callous bunch of men and women. Hey, they were scouts. They had to be. It was a rough callous job. Even so, there were no jokes about Parkerson, O'Gotti and Ben Dillinger. You don't joke about the dead. Only the living are fair game.

The other crews didn't know enough about the failed mission to be able to use the worm-phobia joke. However, one of them left a toy hedgehog in MacEscobar's locker. They had a good laugh when the victim gasped loudly and went visibly pale on opening the door. The joke, coming from a bunch of humans who had little imagination and no originality, was: *How many Skatzochoirophobics does it take to run a desk? Just one, and his name is…*

~~~

This morning MacEscobar gives a little sigh, as the news comes in that yet another colonised planet has imploded and has been left a lifeless clinker. Well, that really should not happen to Brobdingnag, says MacEscobar; there's a world we ought to leave to run its own evolutionary course, thank you very much.

His comrades laugh at him and tell him he must be joking.

He shakes his head while staring into the middle distance, his eyes dead as cinders. He shivers involuntarily and makes a peculiar humming sound. His thoughts are back on the world where he lost his whole crew. Despite the mocking of the others present, MacEscobar has made up his mind that neither commerce nor conquest works when colonising certain planets. For example, in the case of Brobdingnag, a world crawling with ten quintillion insects armed with pincers and stings the size of eagles' talons, the most sensible thing to do was walk on by.

Rán

As a warrior-rower on an Ostmen warship, I was surely looking at an early death. There were several events, natural or manmade, that could take me. A freak storm, a battle, exhaustion, a severe whipping, an execution, a captain who had upset one of the gods, a shipwreck on a shoal, or some other hidden danger. Look, I could go on but you understand. The only way I was going to see any of my children grow up was if I changed my trade, which was in the hands of my superiors. My current betters were a nasty bunch of thickheads, so that wasn't going to happen soon, and it was because their skulls were thick that I ended up in a net with a shoal of dead crewmates – instead of in Valhalla.

We had been to Dyflin on the island of Eire and then recrossed the Celtic Sea to fight Angles in Beornice. We were very fatigued. Hence, we were on our way home, making the crossing over the narrow waters to Jutland, a country ruled by Gorm the Old, when we were hit by the big waterspout. Most of us realised this was an unnatural phenomenon since it came from nowhere: no high wind, no tidal surge, no meeting of fast swells. It simply rose up, a tower of angry silver foam, out of a calm and happy sea, to spin the ship round and round in a far-from-merry dance, flinging all on board into the water.

The first to die was the drummer, he who beats out the rhythm with which the oarsmen have to keep their rowing time. He was cast high in the air and came down stomach first on the point of the mast. His gargling form squirmed and flopped there like a banner caught in crosswinds until the ship disappeared beneath the waves. The rest of us were struggling to keep afloat in the cold sea. Naturally, those who couldn't swim were the first to drown. If they hadn't struggled so violently with their ineptitude they might have survived, for their bodies immediately bobbed up to the surface.

The rest of us kept buoyant for as long as our endurance lasted, then one by one my companions succumbed, and I was the last left alive when a gigantic outstretched arm surfaced with a net in its hand. This was flung over the floating dead, which were hauled below. I was taken with them, kicking and squirming, fighting the mesh. Pale staring bodies were heaped against me, pallid fleshy lips pressed against mine. It's not enjoyable to kiss a dead man who is bloated and spongy from being in the water for age.

Once under the water I saw the owner of the great arm and knew her instantly from campfire stories. It was Rán, the ocean's giantess. She was standing on the shoulders of one of her wave-daughters. This superb goddess was wearing rusty chainmail covered in crustaceans. Crabs and other creatures swarmed in legions over her form. Her eyes were the deep green of kelp, her long floating hair the colour of sea-smoothed amber, her skin a pearly almost-translucent hue. The wife of Aegir was a formidable woman, who caused any desire in a mortal man's loins to shrivel under the glare of her fierce expression. She was beautiful in a full-blooded way, not pretty or demure, no frills or fussiness, just absolute magnificence. You knew she would devour you alive afterwards, quicker than a black widow does her mate.

Once we were all in her net, she submerged, dragging her catch behind her. Fortunately for me in a very short time we were in an airy undersea cavern. I gasped and gulped, before being tipped out of the net onto a rocky shelf. There the monstrous Rán began sorting through the sailors, sucking their souls from their dead bodies and tossing the waste meat to the waiting fish. When her fingers got to me I began wriggling. She held me up to gaze into my terrified face saying in a voice full of disgust, 'A live one!'

I was thrown out into the ball of bodies which were feeding a whole variety of marine life. I felt myself being nibbled by small mouths, but then a maiden suddenly appeared and yanked me back to the cave. At the time I didn't know her name, but later found out it was Kolga, one of Rán's nine daughters.

'Mine!' cried my beautiful saviour. 'I want him.'

~~~

So, I became the lover of a goddess of the sea. Admittedly, she was one of the minor immortals, like Idunn or Lofn, but still a deity to be reckoned with. She spent much of her time keeping me safe, away from her sisters: Bára, Blóðughadda, Bylgja, Dúfa, Hefring, Himinglæva, Hrǫnn and Unnr. I greatly appreciated her jealousy since sharing a seaweed bed with just one of these maids was an exhausting experience. I was expected to maintain an erection nightly and service Kolga with enough passion and enthusiasm to ward off her anger.

I realised that once she became bored with me, I would be meat for the fishes, like my brothers, whose bones now littered the ocean floor.

Thankfully, the daughters were called upon to do other duties, like wrecking ships and boats full of warriors, fishermen, and any other craft on the waters above. In their watery domain they were in human or half-fish form, but once on the surface of the sea they became waves. They smashed vessels to tinder or crashed upon rocky shorelines creating havoc to clifftop dwellings. Daughters of destruction, they came home laughing and giggling, speaking happily of the men, women and children they had drowned or boats they had sunk. Even my dear Kolga, who I'd come to love deeply in my undersea prison, was no different. In fact they had no more compassion than did male gods.

There's a thing I must explain or try to. The cavern was full of air, yet it was under the ocean. I didn't understand why the water did not rush in and fill the open space, especially since there was an exit high above through which I could see the sky. I could only think this magical space was like that of Asgard, home of the great Odin and the other gods. Indeed, the moon was a magical ball of gold or silver, which just hung in the air with no support, so why shouldn't a cavern under the sea be able to hold back the water. Things are what they are, not what they're expected to be. A bird flies through the air, a fish lives under the water without needing to breathe, a snake moves across the ground having no legs. These are all wonders, so why not one more.

Now, I knew I was merely a plaything of the goddess Kolga, but I had to try to satisfy her, both emotionally and physically. Once I was of no more use to her she would either hand me over to her sisters, one or two of whom were monstrously cruel, or she would kill me. I had no easy task, for Kolga was twice as tall as I am, and very impatient. I used my hands skilfully enough, but when she wanted penetration I had to be there like lightning or be thrown out of the cave into the water. There were big fish lurking around the entrance of the cave, so I had to get back quickly. I was a pendulum that swung between ecstasy and terror. I could have kept a dozen clocks wound up sunset to sunset.

One day Rán came and said to Kolga, 'I'm taking your toy away for a while. I need it.'

'What for?' said Kolga, pouting.

This I wanted to hear also. If it was for the same exercises that I performed for Kolga, I was lost. Rán was five times the size of her daughter. I could not imagine any scene where I would be able to give her carnal satisfaction and still retain some dignity and honour. I may be only a rower of a longship, but I am also a fighter with a warrior's pride in his manhood. I could not imagine a situation where I was a laughingstock and allowed myself to live.

I was relieved when Rán replied, 'I need to put colour back in my hair.'

Now, you'll know as well as I do that even if a woman be either the mightiest of warriors or the demurest of pretty creatures, her hair is often her crowning glory. A man can be proud of his hair too. Look at the names of some of our fiercest warrior chiefs: Sven Forkbeard, Harald Finehair, Frode Curlhair. A woman does not lose head hair as a man sometimes does. It is worn like a banner the whole of her life. Important to both sexes, but chiefly to women.

Now that I was staring at Rán's magnificently abundant tresses, I could see the colour had faded. Her curled locks were no longer that beautiful amber hue I witnessed on first seeing her. There was a tinge of hoar frost at the tips. A slight muddiness at the roots. I was therefore intrigued to know how I, a simple mortal, would be able to assist in replenishing what had seeped away into the currents of the ocean. I was certainly no good at anything more than braiding pigtails or topknots, a service we Ostmen did for our closest companions.

'How may I help?' I said to Rán. 'I will do my best.'

She looked down at me as if were a jellyfish that had somehow slipped into her cave and was littering the floor.

'You will learn soon enough,' she replied. 'We are going on a long journey through several seas and oceans, and when we get to our destination I will need you to go where I cannot, onto to the earth, over dry land.'

So, I thought excitedly, a chance to escape.

'And if you try to run away,' she added, 'I will call on all the gods of Asgard to make your life an unremitting misery, to punish you with the most venomous and unspeakable of tortures. You will wish not only that you had not been born, but that death was so close you can touch it.'

'Oh, your godliness,' I said, 'my life is a jewel.'

'Climb on my shoulders and wrap your legs around my neck,' she ordered, 'and if I feel there's any sign of you getting erotic satisfaction from that position I shall stop, take you down and snap it off. Am I clear?'

'Perfectly. I'm sure there's no chance of that... Of course, you are the most sensual of creatures but I am made of iron. I can control my urges.'

I did as I was ordered and we sped off, first up to

the surface and then across it going towards the setting of the sun. Rán remained prone just below the surface of the sea, while I sat upright on her enormous neck, exposed to the world and the sky. I believed this was because if she fully emerged from the water she would lose human form. To outward eyes it no doubt seemed that I was riding on the back of some great whale. The sun and the wind felt good on my body as I streamed along, sometimes passing the odd vessel, those aboard gawping, then signing to ward off evil.

One time we swept past a small fishing boat with a single crew.

'Tell my mother,' I yelled, 'that…' But the rest of my words were lost to the wind.

Once land came in sight we turned left, going at right angles to the setting sun. We ploughed down into wild freezing waters. I lay forward and buried myself in Rán's hair, gathering what warmth I could from her thick locks. She had no need to warn me about getting an erection from our contact for I was useless as a wet piece of seaweed at that point. However, in a short period of time we were going round a cape and up into warmer waters.

My concern then turned to the presence of sharks, seeing black fins cutting the surface of the sea. However, we were going far too swiftly for them and any in our way were swallowed by Rán as if they were sardines.

I cannot count the fish I saw on that journey: spotted whale sharks; great rays that sometimes skimmed the surface; gentle fragile nautiluses going wither the waves took them; huge jellyfish with monstrously long tentacles; giant squids which attempted to snatch me off my perch; whales, of course, and schools of dolphins; wonderous, fantastical life.

Finally, after a long journey over a warm ocean full of small green islands, we came to a large archipelago. Rán took me to the shoreline of a deep wide bay and said, 'You see that fine palace of wood, with its gardens of trees in full blossom? That's the home of an oriental emperor. In those gardens are pools full of fish they call koi carp. They are of many colours; I want you to steal those with gold skins and bring them to me. You may have to go on several trips since I need as many as will give me back the colour of my hair.'

She looked into my eyes after she had given me my instructions and read my thoughts exactly.

'You are thinking you can now escape from Rán.' She shook her terrible head. 'My poor little mortal. The people of these islands *hate* foreigners. Any that wash up on these shores are put to death. You may see some heads of shipwrecked or marooned sailors on spiked posts. If you are seen, all you will hear is the swish of the sword blade that decapitates you.'

'Oh,' I said.

'Now, once it is dark, you must do my bidding.'

So, when the moon rose I set off with a net. I travelled quickly, my eyes open for any man who might be out at night. Indeed, there were strangely dressed guards at the palace gates, in robes and headgear I had never seen before. They wore double-handed swords with black hilts in long curved scabbards. I felt my own burly Ostmen companions could easily dispatch these warriors, who appeared to be small, light and lean creatures.

I found a wall and climbed it, dropping into a garden of such moonlit beauty it took my breath away. The trees and bushes were exquisite, covered with perfumed blossoms that drove me crazy after months of only smelling rotting seaweed. In between groves of trees were pools shining like silver mirrors in the moonbeams which fell across them. I found one of these full of large golden carp and swiftly filled the net with their wriggling forms.

As I was leaving, a moon-shadow fell upon the surface of the water. I froze as a person, a man or a woman I knew not which, wandered over and stared into the water. Once the moonlight caught his face I could see by his small black beard he was a man. I was heartily relieved he had not seen me among the trees, seeming to be in a reverie. Perhaps he was some lovelorn swain? He was so wrapped in his thoughts I don't think he noticed that many of the precious carp were missing. Finally, with a heartfelt sigh he left the place, the hem of his elegant beautiful gown, a garment decorated with silver and gold images in its shining folds, swishing the mown grass of the lawn.

When I got back to Rán, she took the fish eagerly and swallowed them one by one. In the next hour her hair, floating on the surface of the sea, began to take on that amber sheen which was her pride and delight. It was yet not quite as magnificent as it had been, but the process had begun. I was both amazed and relieved, for had it not worked I think I would have followed the koi down her gullet and into that whale-sized stomach.

'You did well,' she told me. 'I am pleased.'

'They'll think the fish have been stolen by herons,' I told her, 'which is good for me, since they'll be seeking the thieves at dawn. Herons don't normally raid pools at night. They wait for first light.' I continued in an aggrieved tone, 'I've lost many a fish to such sly birds.'

I slept the next day in a cave by the shore, aware that if I was caught by the inhabitants of this strange island I would be executed.

The following three nights I made the same trip, though on the third there were far more people about in the gardens. I guessed this was because they had at last noticed the missing carp and had been watchful for herons that never came. They had probably deduced that the thief was an animal or a human. The guards carried paper lanterns and in their light I could see bows and quiversful of arrows. The moon had gone behind thick cloud that night and I knew by instinct and feel which way to go to the pond I wanted, so I simply waited for a dark passage with no lanterns and made my way to the golden pool. There I worked by feel, standing knee-deep in the water and waiting for a carp to brush my leg, before reaching down and snatching it out of its domain.

Suddenly, two lanterns appeared out of the darkness, close together. I crouched down low near to the water, my netful of golden koi close to my chest. Fortunately, the lanterns remained in the bushes a few ells distance from the pool. There were whispers and caresses. In the lamplight I could see it was the same man I'd seen sighing deeply three nights ago as he stared down into the koi pool. With him was with a woman in a beautiful shining gown. He was stroking her soft-looking cheeks and murmuring in her ear.

This was all I needed: a pair of lovers!

They were so enwrapped with each other they failed to notice me. I remained as still as a heron prior to stabbing fish. All through the gardens the lanterns were floating hither and thither as guards scoured the area for intruders. Then as I watched the man's hand went under the folds of his lover's robe and a moment later she let out a passionate moan of delight.

In the next moment a large, portly man came out of darkness without a lantern in his hand. He yanked the two figures apart. Then there was a flash in the lamplight as his sword came out. The next second a head was rolling on the grass with a surprised expression on its face. The robe with the body in it crumpled and collapsed to the ground. A scream shattered the silence.

The stout man began shouting at the woman, who started weeping and wailing. I imagined her tormentor was her husband or father. Unfortunately, while he was waiting for a reply the fish in my net suddenly began thrashing noisily, seeking escape. The man looked up and saw me crouched in a ball. He stared for a moment then pointed and yelled. Swiftly, for a fat man encumbered by heavy robes, he sheathed his bloody blade and unslung his bow.

I leapt out of the pond and began my escape, my net of gold over my shoulder. An arrow buried its point in my topknot. I continued running, not bothering to pull it out, reached the wall and climbed it as swift as a weasel going up a tree for eggs. Another arrow struck the parapet as I jumped down to the earth on the other side. I fled across the landscape to the beach, aware that my assailant was close behind. How did such a porker manage to run and climb as fast as me, a lithe and muscled Ostmen? Yet there he was, some thirty ells behind me and gaining. Normally I would have turned and faced him and allowed combat, but he had that bloody bow, and even without that I had seen him cut off a man's head quicker than the eye could follow. He was a deadly warrior, disciplined, fit and swift, and very skilled with his weapons.

On the shoreline, he was about ten ells behind me. He would have caught me if Rán had not intervened. A forceful wave, Rán in her symbolic form, came surging up the beach and took my opponent off his feet, slamming him against a large granite rock. He burst like a giant rotten turnip, his innards splattering the shingle. Rán quickly flowed back to her preferred habitat.

There were other local warriors now, close behind him, yelling and firing arrows which fell short. I rushed into the ocean, found my saddle on Rán's neck, and we slipped away into the darkness of the sea. Rán quickly gained speed and we were on our way home, travelling in a different way from that which we had come, in order to make a complete circle of the world.

We had several adventures on the way back, which I won't bore you with since they were repeats of our journey to the island. Rán's hair was now back to its wondrous amber hue and she was well pleased. I asked if I could be allowed to leave her as we passed by the isle of Eire. She refused, saying she had promised Kolga that I would be returned to her unharmed. I was bereft at this news, though a plan formed in my head.

We Ostmen had built a city on Eire Island which we called Dyflin and the Irish people called Duiblinn. We had established ourselves on that island because the oak trees there were excellent for building our longships. When I was last in Dyflin I drank mead with some Irishmen who called themselves 'monks'. They called me 'pagan' and told me they worshipped a god who needed no name. They told me there was only one true God.

'One god? I'd replied. 'That's surely not enough. We have Odin and a whole host of gods to assist and guide us through life.'

'Ah, but do they make your life worth living?' came back the monks, 'or are they more trouble than they're worth?'

I shrugged, not knowing how to answer, without leaving me with the worry of being punished by at least one of Odin's horde.

'Ours is the one true God,' said one of the monks, 'and if you believe in Him all other false gods will vanish swifter than the mist before the sun on yonder peat bog. You simply have to believe, have faith in the truth. Your gods are only in your head, not in your heart. Some of your people have realised that and have become followers of our Faith and have shed their paganism.'

At the time I'd scoffed at this theory and scorned those of my fellow warriors who'd abandoned their old beliefs. Now, however, I saw this conversion might be useful to me. No gods are real if they're not taken seriously. They only exist if they're recognised and worshipped.

While on the journey back to the underwater cavern I bent my mind to the task of recognising the truth of the monks' words. I forced myself to mentally discard my belief in those gods with whom I'd grown to manhood and told myself that this god of the Irish monks was the only real deity in the universe, even though he did not approve of pillage and slaughter. That part took a lot of mental effort, since I wondered how I was going make a living if killing and robbing weaker tribes was not permitted. However, I had been born with a very strong mind, one that could bend facts into fiction if necessary.

Sure enough, as we passed Eire I put a magnitude of effort into my task of renouncing my pagan gods and in accepting the one God of the Irish monks. Rán slid away from under me, to disappear into the depths of the ocean, leaving me floating on the surface. I struck out in a strong swim for the shore and managed to reach it without drowning. I could have put this down to my new saviour and given thanks to that Lord, but instead I reverted to my old ways. I gave thanks to Njǫrd instead, knowing that my old trade of raiding and plundering, sacking villages and towns, was under threat if I didn't.

After all, I was no monk and never would be, no matter how much I tried. They were dedicated men of pen and parchment, spending their lives illuminating letters that meant nothing to me. I was a son of the axe and sword, and my ink was pools of blood. I couldn't read or write and what's more most of those monks were celibate. I couldn't do without a woman to keep me warm on cold winter nights, the soft brush of her willing mound pressed against my thigh, bringing the stiffening heat rushing into my loins.

I had escaped my fate. A giant goddess had caged me and yet I'd found a way out of my watery prison. I waited for the vengeance Rán had promised if I ran away, but it never came. I think she was pleased with my assistance with the golden carp and had decided not to call the wrath of the gods upon my head. I was as free as an ocean fish.

Yet I miss my beautiful Kolga and yesterday I went down to the edge of the sea. There I immersed my legs and hips in the surf that lapped the shore in gentle rhythmic wavelets. I have learned by my escape, from

Kolga's mother, that imagination is a very powerful tool. I closed my eyes and let the wavelets wash repeatedly around my nether parts. I swear by Odin's escorts, by his wolves and ravens, that Kolga came to me in wave after wave to caress my body again – and again – oh, oh, oh, yes, and again…

Giant

When I was younger, perhaps eight years of age, I had long black hair – iron black – that fell straight to my ankles. I was slim and dark-eyed in those days (even the eyes have changed to a watery-red – some disease carried by the dust, they tell me); and I could *run*. Oh yes, I could run faster than a gazelle, and I thought that was to be my role in life: to be a runner, a messenger for the king. I would have liked that. I am, by nature, a quiet man, solitary. You won't find a more peaceful man in the whole of Palestine. It would have suited me to have been out on the plains, alone, with some important note from a king, to a king, in my hand.

There's something very inviting about being unencumbered by the trappings of war – the heavy armour and weapons that have plagued me throughout my life – that's good for the soul. The sandals and loin cloth of a runner allow not just your body but also your *spirit* to breathe. You feel free *inside* as well as out. Running between cities, too, somehow severs your relationship with them. I would have been as free as the animals of the dusty plains.

Runners get to meet a lot of important people. Not just their own king but others as well. Of course, it can be a dangerous business when a royal-this insults a royal-that, and you're the one carrying the poisonous words; but what occupation is completely free of danger these days? Being a messenger can also be a rewarding job. The birth of a child, the marriage of a son or daughter, the death of a tyrant – these are all good news, entitling the bearer to all sorts of fine gifts, from baskets of figs to gold amulets.

Yes, I should like to have been a runner. I did begin as such, within the city of Gath, but as I put on weight and more height I became slower, and realised that running was a career that I was growing out of, literally.

How the other children taunted me about my height! I had my hair cut because it looked so stupid – this tall shambling creature trailing a long mane of hair. The jibes still came though, and not very original. Jokes about ice behind my ears and to be careful when eagles were about, looking for places to nest. How they wounded me, those catcalls, yet I smiled through them, good-naturedly. What else can you do? It's always supposed that a tall person is good at fighting, but that's not true. Height, even strength, do not make a good fighter. Warriors are born, not made. Those who love a battle arrive in this world with a chip of ice lodged in their heart, or fire in their guts, and they are usually naturals when it comes to weaponry. Sometimes they carry a grievance against mankind, which manifests itself in viciousness.

Anyway, they have the killer instinct, the will to win, which I do not. You've either got it, or you haven't. You can't fake it and you can't make it. It's there, or it isn't. A goatherd might have it and a king might not. That's the way it goes and it's no use whining about it.

I was neither hot-headed nor did I hate my fellow men. Any skills at war I had to learn the hard way. I was clumsy and had no enthusiasm for ways of the sword and was consequently not very good at it. Of course, I learned a certain amount, enough to survive in battle after the first few close shaves, but anyone can do that. One thing I could not do was fight against my friends. That's why I allowed them to taunt me. Hitting a stranger is far easier than striking a companion.

Anyway, I kept on growing until I was an embarrassment, even to my mother. There's always a limit to these things and there came a time when the insults suddenly stopped and were replaced by looks of awe and wariness. I suppose it was about the time that I reached eighteen years, when my shoulders filled out and my limbs began to thicken. I did a lot of lifting in those days: blocks of stone that went into building walls and houses. I could reach higher than most and the builders said (usually with a smile) that they found it cheaper to use me than to erect scaffolding.

I don't want you to get the idea that I was so huge I could touch the rooftops. Nothing of the sort. But I could reach first-floor windows, which none of the other workers could manage. I began to feel a certain pride in myself, for the first time in my life.

In those days I used to do a lot of drinking; building labourers do. I became acceptable to my companions once more, especially since I could drink my quota, and theirs, and carry half the drunks home with me afterwards. I think that was the happiest period in my life. I managed to save enough to buy myself a wife, less than half my size, but she made up for it in brains. She was a very clever woman and unlike many other girls I had asked out, didn't mind being seen with me in the street. She was the fiery type, Rachel. One of those small people with the killer instinct, that I spoke of earlier. She would have made a far better warrior than me. I let her bully me a bit, which amused my friends but they didn't understand. It wasn't necessary to brook her: she knew what was what, and I was quite happy to let her manage our affairs. It was Rachel who said that the slaves being brought into Gath would eventually put me out of work and that it might be wise to seek some other line of employment before all of us were on the streets and there was a glut. I took her advice, of course. She was always right about these things. I joined the army. There wasn't anything else I could do.

Sure enough, that summer our Philistine commanders were more successful than they had ever been, and who needs to pay workers by the week when you can buy them outright?

I was miserable at first, in the army. No one pushed me around anymore, but I found the life hard. The fact that I was big didn't make the armour any lighter. I had to carry twice the amount that a normal man hefts around, and I had to keep it clean too. I would be polishing my breastplate and helmet long after the other soldiers had fallen asleep for the night.

The marching and drilling was loathsome, and I was glad when we were sent out into the field despite the fact that you baked during the day, and the night was cold enough to freeze the water in your goatskins. At least I wasn't banging my head against a beam over a doorway, and out in the open the smells were cleaner and purer. It all seemed so much clearer out there, on the plains. I really envied the runners and the occasional shepherd we passed. They had the best of it. If only I hadn't kept on growing! I comforted myself with the idea that I was closer to the stars and imagined I could reach out and touch them. It would have been a great pleasure to have gathered them in a net and distributed them amongst my companions. Wishful thinking, though. We sweated and choked on the dust thrown up by the wheels of the officers' chariots as they thundered past our ranks. Only the thought of a jug of water from some distant well kept us going.

I was never promoted. Despite that I was strong they never considered me fit for command and passed me over continually. I didn't mind that much. I'm not a great one for discipline. I'll obey orders, of course, but I'm not sure I'd enjoy giving them. You have to be a special sort of man for that. One of those with a chip of ice, because it's a lonely life as a non-commissioned officer. I was already lonely enough as it was without adding to my troubles.

No, I was happier in the ranks – but still, I felt a twinge, just a twinge of envy, when other younger men were offered advancement. Rachel used to nag me about my lack of ambition, but that was Rachel. I knew she was proud of me, whatever I did. It would just have been nice for her to be able to rub something in the noses of her family.

They had never approved of me – a builder's labourer and despite my offer for Rachel (who some do not call pretty) had amounted to more than she had been expected to fetch, large bride prices do not win respect. In fact I got the impression that they despised me for overpaying, thinking it ignorant and vulgar. But as Rachel pointed out, they took the money quickly enough. That's relations for you.

What I didn't like about the army was that you had to kill people. It's a messy business. I was never much good at jabbing with a straight arm. I'm your hacking type – much more useful chopping down at the heads rather than poking at people. Besides, I was much more likely to blind a man – the heart was a bit low for my thrust – and I would hate to think of some poor creature stumbling around in darkness, from city to city, with a begging bowl in his hands, and all because of my inept swordplay. Better to cleave a skull in twain than leave a man without his sight.

I can throw a spear, of course; quite well in fact. But that's a one-off business. If you miss, which is quite likely because they're easy things to dodge, then that's it; you have to go in with the sword anyway. People have been known to miss with javelins in a small room, so I've got little faith in them. Spears are not very reliable in the heat of the battle either. You're just as likely to hit friend as foe. I've got this long heavy shaft with an iron head which I flourish around a lot, but that's mostly for show. A lot of the time I won't even bother with it, once the fighting starts. Pretty useless thing really, unless you lunge with it. Arrows and slingshot stones are much harder to avoid.

They're the things that trouble me: little whizzing bits of wood and stone flying through the air. You can't even see them let alone know when to duck. None of us likes them. The captain said the other day that when we catch a slinger we ought to cut his pebbles off to make him impotent. The other men laughed but I couldn't see the joke. After all, there's nothing funny about missiles you can't see hitting you in the eye or somewhere else just as deadly.

And what glory is there in it? Why do they bother to come to the field at all, when everyone there, even people on their own side, despises them? There's nothing noble about firing into a melee hoping that your random shot will find a mark. Much of the time you can't even see if you've hit anyone, or if a soldier merely tripped or stumbled. Half of those the archers and slingers claim as definite hits get up and walk off the battlefield afterwards, dusting their thighs and complaining about loose greaves. If you're going to be in the fighting, I say, then *be* in it – not half-a-mile away, ready to run if you miss. Cowards, most of these people. They can get within thirty paces of you and still be away like rabbits. They don't wear armour so that doesn't hold them back. Many's the time I tried to put up a chase, but it's hopeless when you're carrying a ton of brass on your back, and the little bastard in front is built like an antelope. But then, that's war for you. Anything goes. There's no rule says you can't hit and run. I've seen more Israeli bottoms than faces, and that's a fact.

~~~

I'm sixty now and getting past it. That surprises you, eh? Sixty? Well, I'm almost bald, except for a grey tuft or two poking under my helmet, and these eyes give me trouble. (I think it *must* be the dust. You can't march about for forty-odd years and not get sore eyes in these lands.) My nose has gone a funny shade of purple and people complain about my gaseous bowels, but I'm still a man to reckon with. Of course, the old bones ache of a cold morning and I have difficulty in bending these days, but *still*, not bad for an old soldier. A few wounds here and there, most of them healed cleanly, but what veteran doesn't have his battle scars to parade before the raw recruits?

Did I mention that Rachel was dead? Last year. Sad, really, since I'm about to retire. This is my last battle. The captain has told me, by this time next month I'll be lying on my back in Gath, sucking grapes. (Not much else you can do when all your teeth have gone, is there?) Rachel died of some lung complaint, poor dear. She didn't let it get her down though. Game to the last. It'll be a lonely retirement without her. We planned a little farm, but now I think I'll move in with her brother. He could use an extra hand in that vineyard of his. These old scarred hands are not good for much these days, except lifting hayricks. They once warmed a frozen sparrow back to life, but that was long ago and not worth mentioning really.

Ah! Four o'clock! The captain's calling for me. I've got to go out into the valley and bellow at the enemy. Poor devils have been cowering there amongst the rocks for days, while I shout my head off and strut around like lord muck. All show really. It was the captain's idea. I think he's bucking for promotion, and anyway, it's nice for me to go out of the army with a bit of flair. There's not been much of that in my life. Strap on the old brass and get out there with a bit of lung power. Nothing to it. Not much chance they'll send anybody down to meet me now. I've been at it for days, without a sign from them. They're enjoying the rest as much as we are.

Of course, there's always the possibility that some squirt with the killer instinct is looking for a quick way up the ladder. There's been one or two rumours lately. I expect old King Saul is having his ear bent by some impatient fool now, but that bit about 'You'll be our slaves, or we'll be your slaves' has kept him in check so far. No one wants that kind of responsibility. Clever of the captain to think of that. Only a complete egotist would risk the slavery of his nation on a single combat. I know *I* shout it but if they'd done it first you wouldn't find me going up to the king and saying, 'Please sir, let me go down and sort him out?' I'm not a quick fellow, but I'm not that dull either. Too much responsibility can slow a man down in times of crisis. There. That's the breastplate on. Where's that fellow that carries the shield for me? Always late. I don't blame him. Bloody boring business, if you ask me, lugging another man's shield around. Quite a new experience for an old warrior like myself to have a shield-bearer. It would have tickled Rachel. All show.

All show. Got to give the spectators something to look at, I suppose.

Ah, here we are. Well, that's it. Be back in time for evening meal. If they *do* send someone out, which is unlikely, it'll be a sweaty business until the sun goes down. It's like an oven in this stuff, and he'll be no better off. So long as it's quick and clean, either way. I shan't be sorry to go. A few clashes with the old blade will work up an appetite for one of us to satisfy. That's the stuff. He'll be quicker than me – they all are these days – but I've still got strength on my side. Sort of evens it out. Makes a fair fight of it.

At least I won't need eyes in the back of my head, looking for those wretched archers and slingers. That's something to be thankful for. Sticks and stones? Not today, I hope.

Ah-ha, someone's stepped forward out of the ranks of the Israelites. A small one, nothing but a boy. What are they thinking of, sending such a weakling? He looks a nice young lad. Handsome, and probably oh so brave. What a pity to have to kill the youth.

But I have to do my duty…